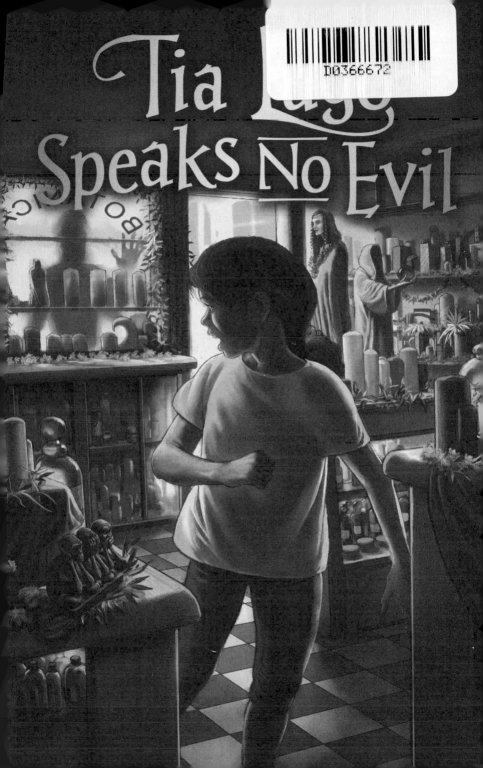

Tia Lugo
Speaks No Evil

# Tia Lugo Speaks No Evil

## Danette Vigilante

JOLLY
FiSH
PRESS
Mendota Heights, Minnesota

First Edition
First Printing, 2021

Book design by Sarah Taplin
Cover design by Sarah Taplin
Cover illustration by Nick Harris (Beehive Illustration)
Dedication page photographs provided by the author

Jolly Fish Press, an imprint of North Star Editions, Inc.

Library of Congress Cataloging-in-Publication Data (pending)
978-1-63163-575-5

Jolly Fish Press
North Star Editions, Inc.
2297 Waters Drive
Mendota Heights, MN 55120
www.jollyfishpress.com

Printed in Canada

*To Sal, my husband, BFF, and partner in crime. Thanks for sharing this life with me. I couldn't do any of it without you by my side.*

*To my girls, Mia and Ami, for not disowning me for my silliness. Remember: whatever I am, you shall become!*

*And lastly, to grandmothers everywhere, because where would any of us be without their love and strength?*

# Chapter One

The world is a dangerous place to live, not because of the people who are evil, but because of the people who don't do anything about it.

*—Albert Einstein*

It looked like we had been robbed. Piles of clothing were strewn across the floor of my small bedroom. Seven sets of flip-flops, three pairs of sandals, and two pairs of sneakers lay in a mismatched heap near the open closet door. Every summer Dad questioned my love of flip-flops, but Mom never did. She totally got it and even had a collection of her own. Mom tried to get Dad to buy a pair, but his response was always the same: "My shoes need to be tied on. Flip-flops make me walk funny." Then he'd laugh and walk away like Frankenstein. Stiff legs, arms stretched out in front. It never failed to crack me up.

The new suitcase Gram bought me sat open on my bed. I'd never owned a suitcase before and had always used a backpack for weekend trips to Gram's small house, which was only five blocks away from ours.

The suitcase was almost too pretty to use. Wrapped around the entire case was a picture of a sun-drenched forest. In the scene, tree branches glowed in the sunlight, casting long shadows on the ground below them. The picture made me think of woodland animals and mythological creatures. It was perfect for the occasion, but especially fitting for my destination. The next day my parents were going to drive me to sleepaway camp, where there'd be plenty of trees. Camp Troy was three hours away from home and was, according to its website, "nestled in a wealth of pure beauty" and promised to be "the foundation for an extraordinary summer."

The New York City Parks Department sponsored Camp Troy. This year the camp's focus was wilderness survival skills. I really wanted to attend, especially after reading *Lost in the River of Grass*. It was a book about a girl my age who took a weekend trip to the Everglades and found herself lost for three days with hardly any food or water.

Of course, normal activities were available at Camp Troy, too, like swimming lessons in the lake, roasting marshmallows, sitting around the campfire, hiking, and putting on shows. But I was more excited about learning survival skills, like how to properly use a map and compass and how to tell the difference between berries that were okay to eat and ones that would knock you dead. Basically, I wanted to learn everything I'd never had the opportunity to experience living in the city.

I had begged my parents all winter to let me go and when they'd finally said yes, that's when my nerves went berserk. Other than staying at Gram's, I'd never been away from my parents overnight. It was like with all of my begging I'd been pulling on a rubber band, and when it finally gave way, I had no idea what to do next. Until that point, I hadn't thought it completely through. The camp was way out in the country, and I was pretty sure there'd be lots of snakes plus all sorts of creepy crawlers I'd never seen before. Not only that, but I'd have to share a cabin with five complete strangers. One week could feel like a month if my cabinmates didn't like me. But I knew that no matter what happened, I'd have to suck it up. My parents made sure I knew that unless it was a real emergency—like my asthma acting up—I was going to stay put for a whole week.

As I sat on top of the suitcase, trying to smoosh everything down inside it, there was a knock on my bedroom door.

"Come in," I said.

Julius squeezed by me and the bulging suitcase. "Hey," he said. "Almost done packing?"

Julius, my best friend, was the only person I knew whose eyes changed color. Sometimes they were green, other times light brown. That day they were green, my favorite. He'd always been the cutest guy in our neighborhood and in school.

Julius's short, silky hair was as black and shiny as fresh tar and refused to do anything but lie straight on his head. He kept it parted to the side and used hairspray and gel to keep it from flopping into his eyes.

I shook my head, then pointed to the flip-flop mountain. "I still have to squeeze those in somewhere."

"Are you supplying your cabinmates too?"

"Very funny. I need a different pair for each day. Now come help me."

Julius crammed five pairs of flip-flops and one pair of sandals in the outside pockets of the suitcase.

"Sorry, that's all that'll fit," he said.

DANETTE VIGILANTE

"It's okay, I'll wear my sneakers there and stick the rest of the flip-flops into my hoodie pockets."

Julius sat on the floor beside me, his long skinny legs stretched out before him. "You're so lucky, T," he said. "I wish I were going too. You excited?"

"Yeah, I'm super excited. I can't believe the day is almost here." I stopped struggling with the suitcase and began fanning myself. "I'm a little nervous though. I mean, it's a whole week. What if the food is really gross or one of my cabinmates snores like a moose? Or worse, I get the top bunk and fall off in front of everyone?"

"Hmm," Julius said. "What if the sky falls too?"

"You got jokes today, huh?"

Julius laughed, then added, "Seriously, I'm sure the snacks will be good at least, and you can always pack earplugs. And the bed? Just make sure you claim a bottom bunk as soon as you can. Like, fling a pair of flip-flops onto it or something."

Julius flung an invisible Frisbee into the air, which made me laugh, and I suddenly felt much better.

After a little while, Julius softly nudged his knee into mine. "I'm going to miss you."

The spot where his knee touched mine grew warm and I couldn't bring myself to look at him. "I'm going to miss you too, Jul."

It wasn't until then that I realized being away from Julius was one of the things I was worried about.

Julius looked at the time on his phone. "I have to go," he said. "I promised Mom I'd clean my room today."

10

We both stood, then Julius grabbed me for a quick hug. "I'll bring your suitcase to the front door for you so you won't have to do it in the morning when you leave."

I watched him go, lugging my suitcase behind him, and almost wished I'd never heard of Camp Troy.

That night, it was impossible to fall asleep, and when I finally did, it was only to be awakened at 3:00 a.m. when that familiar breathing-through-a-straw feeling struck. My lungs squeezed smaller and tighter and demanded more air. As I reached for my inhaler, I tried my best to stay calm, but failed. My heart slammed against my rib cage like it wanted out.

My fingers trembled and instead of grabbing the inhaler, I accidentally sent it flying off the night table. It skidded across the floor, barely making a sound. I tried not to move too fast as I got out of bed. I had learned the hard way that it was better to stay calm when my asthma acted up. Well, easier said than done.

The imaginary straw I breathed through became even smaller as my lungs demanded more air. My upper back hurt, too, sometimes that happened when my lungs worked overtime.

I probably should've woken up my parents, but I didn't want to freak them out. They might change their minds about Camp Troy. If Mom thought I might be having trouble breathing, she'd want to rush me into the ER, where we would spend most of the night counting oxygen levels. The ER can be scary sometimes too. Once, the cops brought in four guys who were in a street fight. They were bloody and loud. One guy wasn't even wearing a shirt. The gash on his back looked deep and painful. Dad stood in front of me so I wouldn't have to see, but he couldn't do anything about the nasty things the man said to the doctors and nurses, like it was their fault he was there and not his.

On my hands and knees, I finally found my inhaler near the window, almost completely hidden behind a stack of old books that I just couldn't seem to get rid of. My bedroom would make hoarders everywhere proud.

After I emptied my lungs as much as possible, I pumped the inhaler once, sucked down the miracle mist, then held it in and forced it deep into my ailing lungs until I couldn't anymore. One puff would make things better, but two would completely banish the invisible beast that sat on my chest. So, I pumped again.

I'd always thought of my inhaler as a lion tamer, only in my case it was more of a lung tamer. I'd heard that some kids outgrew their asthma, but since I was already thirteen, I knew my chances of that were slim.

I stood and sipped from a bottle of water on my night table to the right side of my bed, near the window. I pulled the gauzy white curtain aside, looking out into the night as I waited for the medicine to kick in.

It was a clear night, the kind I loved—dark blue like velvet, with more stars dotted across the sky than usual.

I looked down to the sidewalk, and at first, I wasn't sure what I saw. I thought maybe I was having some kind of hallu-cination. I mean, my lungs felt like they were stuffed with big fluffy cotton balls, so there had to be a serious lack of oxygen to my brain. I figured a brain short on air on a humid July night was more than capable of holding some kind of weird power over the rest of my body. But no, not mine. My brain just kept on seeing truths as clear as Gram's fancy crystal water glasses. That truth was a man lying facedown on the bloody cement sidewalk. The truth didn't stop there either. Another unfamiliar man, dressed in dark pants and a hoodie, knelt over him. He held a knife.

The light from the streetlamp caught the blade and sent a momentary gleam into the night. Maybe he had heard me as I wheezed.

Shocked, I trembled like it was the middle of February. I'd never felt anything like this in my life. Even my insides quaked and stirred up the dinner I had eaten hours before.

I tried to convince myself that it was all a sick prank, and that the man who lay on the ground would get up and laugh it off. At least that was what I prayed for. But when that didn't happen, I ripped my cell phone from the nearby charger and began to enter the passcode. My hands shook like crazy, but when I finally got it right, I made the mistake of looking back to the shadowy stranger below. My face had been lit up by my phone screen. If he looked up, he'd be able to see me clearly. Even though I knew this, I couldn't make myself move. No matter how many times my mind screamed for me to step away from the window, my bare feet wouldn't budge.

The man used his foot to nudge the hooded figure lying in a growing pool of blood. When the man on the ground didn't move, I began to dial 911, but the phone slipped from my quivering hands before I had finished dialing. That's when the man looked up directly at me and held a finger to his lips. I stumbled backward. I never took my eyes off the knife.

"Oh no," I whispered.

In my mind, I heard his "hush" loud and clear. It became a part of me, and I knew if I didn't keep the man's secret, I'd die too. If he could hurt a grown man, permanently silencing a thirteen-year-old girl would be easy. Still, I thought about trying to call 911 again, but the giant pool of blood around the man and the stillness of his body told me that I was already too late to save him.

Little by little, I drew the curtain closed but left it open just enough to peek through. At the very least, I thought, maybe the stranger would think he hallucinated too.

The killer looked one last time in my direction, shooting a glare up to my window, then took off. And just like that, the world I knew was shattered.

I stayed at the window a few minutes longer and numbly stared out into the night. Seeing, but not comprehending.

When I got back into bed, nothing was the same. The room somehow felt bigger—or maybe I was smaller; I didn't know. Even the air was thicker and warmer, and time seemed to slow my every move. It was like someone had carved a hole in the universe and tossed me into space.

With each blink, the scene outside my window glowed like an X-ray on the insides of my eyelids. I squeezed my eyes shut tighter and tighter, but nothing got rid of the image. I sat on the edge of my bed and punched the pillow until my arms ached.

Finally, I buried my face into the pillow. "No," I screamed

like a prayer, until my throat felt raw. No for the man who had been hurt. No for the man with the knife. No to being threatened. No to being changed forever because I knew I'd miss the girl I was before tonight.

I'm not sure how long it was before my lungs eased themselves back to normal, but when they did, I quietly slipped into Mom and Dad's room. I stood silently in the doorway and listened to the sound of their unworried breathing. It was like they were part of a team I no longer belonged to, and I felt jealous. I was alone and would have to stay that way so that they could continue to live in that peaceful, untroubled world. I could never tell them what I saw, I realized, remembering the murderer's echoing "hush."

When I wiggled between my parents, something I hadn't done since I was little, Mom absentmindedly patted my leg. "It was just a bad dream, Tia," she said, "*todo está bien.*"

I wondered if Mom would've still believed all would be well if she knew what had brought me to her bed.

Gram once told me that God never needed to hear actual words, that if you spoke to him with your mind and heart, he'd hear you. Still, as I willed myself to sleep, I whispered one last prayer. "Please, please, keep me safe."

# Chapter Two

The next morning, I found myself back in my room. Sometime during the night Dad must've gotten tired of hanging off his side of the bed and brought me back.

Mrs. Pérez, the lady who lived across the street from us in a small house with a bubblegum-pink front door, woke me up at 6:30 a.m. by talking to the neighborhood women directly beneath my window. The memory from the night before immediately resurrected.

I heard the police say the man probably died in less than five minutes. That with so much blood, an artery must've been severed.

"No one even saw it happen," Mrs. Pérez said, her Spanish accent curling around each word.

What Mrs. Pérez didn't know was that someone *did* see and that someone was me.

I couldn't trust myself to stay silent, so I used both hands to cover my mouth. I wasn't sure what would come out—a sob, a scream, or a confession that I had seen the killer—but "shhhh" was what he ordered, so that's what I cowardly gave him.

Snickering and chatter that I couldn't hear clearly drifted up from below, so I peeked out the window.

Mrs. Patterson, Mrs. Russo, and Mrs. Pérez quieted as

they watched a woman photograph the man's body. He was still splayed facedown on the sidewalk. A white sheet lay next to him. I counted four plainclothes policemen plus seven uniformed officers as they searched the area. All faces were grim and resolute.

Large blue letters on the side of a white police van parked close by read *NYPD Crime Scene*.

My eyes lingered on the police activity a little longer before I gave myself permission to really see the man on the ground.

The body wasn't twisted abnormally or rolled into a fetal position like you see in movies, but there was something eerie about its stillness. It was almost as if the air around the body stood frozen in time, waiting to be released somehow.

The cement near him was no longer light gray like it had always been. A large reddish-brown stain surrounded him in a sickly, shiny puddle. His head was twisted to the side and prevented me from seeing his face. I was grateful for that. I didn't want to know if his eyes were open or closed, or worse— looking up, lifelessly, at me. But with the wave of thankfulness, my stomach tightened with guilt.

Every hair on my head tingled at the root.

My stomach lurched again, and I thought I might heave whatever I had in it all over the windowsill. Luckily, the feeling passed quickly.

When the woman was done, she covered the man with the sheet. Soon after, the neighborhood women picked up their conversation where they had left off.

"Don't mind that one," Mrs. Russo said to Mrs. Patterson.

Then she lowered her voice and added, "Carmella Pérez is what we call a know-it-all."

Mom said sometimes people pretended to be something they weren't because there were things missing from their lives and they were trying to fill in the empty space.

I wondered what was absent from Mrs. Pérez's life, then I wished bravery wasn't missing from mine.

I desperately wanted to hear more of what the ladies had to say, but Dad knocked on the door and interrupted my eaves-dropping. I hopped back into bed just before he entered.

Dad stepped into the room. "Tia?" he said. "The commotion woke you too?"

"What? No. I had a bad dream, that's all," I said, panicked. I thought he meant what happened in the middle of the night rather than what had been going on outside.

"I know, Mom told me. I'm talking about the noise out there." He pointed toward the window. "Is it the reason you're up so early? You're not due at camp for another four hours."

*Camp.* There was no way I could leave now. I thought it'd be cool to learn how to survive in the wilderness, but suddenly survival had taken on a different meaning. The murderer had made sure of that. I had to stay close to home and my parents if I wanted to survive for real.

"I . . . I decided not to go," I said, glad my room was only bathed in the soft morning light. If it hadn't been, Dad would've seen the threatening tears.

Dad quickly made his way to me and felt my forehead. "What? Why? Are you sick?"

"No, I just think it's a waste of time." I forced a small laugh. "I mean, when will I ever need to know how to survive in the wild?"

I couldn't read Dad's face in the dim light, but I knew he didn't buy my story.

"Maybe I'll do something else, like volunteer at the library," I said. "At least I'll get to read all the good books first. That's more useful, right?"

Dad studied me for another minute. "I'm okay with whatever you'd like to do this summer, but let me talk to Mom about it."

"Okay," I said.

Dad kissed my cheek. "Mom and I are going out to see what's going on. We'll only be a few minutes."

I could've saved my parents the trip and filled them in on what happened, but there was no way I could talk to them or anyone about what I saw. I just wanted it all to quietly disappear.

Maybe, if I kept the secret silently tucked away, eventually it would get smaller and smaller, until one day I would be able to convince myself it was nothing more than a bad dream brought on by struggling lungs and an oxygen-starved brain. Then, keeping quiet wouldn't even qualify as a lie, which was a good thing, because Gram said she can see a lie in anyone's eyes before it even comes out of their mouth. That's one of the things she visited the botanica, a spiritual store, for. She bought special incense and candles that kept lies in her sight and evil away. Gram said she once saw the botanica referred to as the "Home Depot of spirituality."

The store sold mystical and religious items like saint statues, candles, incense, oils, and other stuff. People used those things for everything from healing to attracting love, but Gram said it went beyond that. Growing up in Puerto Rico, her family had always been involved with a botanica, and her mom and *abuela* had even considered it to be part of their religion. I saw it differently. How could God want you to make use of all those man-made objects? I wasn't a believer, and neither was Dad. He said botanicas were for desperate people who searched for miracles and quick fixes to their problems, and I agreed. Dad and Gram had gone head-to-head over this about a zillion times, but I never let on how I felt. I never wanted to hurt Gram's feelings, but the botanica had always been something I needed to hide from the outside world. It was embarrassing.

Dad said Gram wasted her money at the botanica. Money that she really didn't have. She bought other stuff, too, like different herbs that were supposed to cure you of sicknesses or oils to rub on your forehead to bring you luck. One time in fourth grade, Gram saw me studying for a math test and quickly applied oil just above my eyebrows.

"A little bit of help never hurt anyone," Gram said.

I opened a bag of potato chips, then continued to hit the books.

When Dad got home from work a little while later, he wiped the oil away. "Whoa," he said. "Those chips are super greasy."

Gram had already left, taking the special oil with her.

Once Gram made me a special herb tea for my asthma. The

rim of the mug had just touched my lips when Dad marched into the kitchen and took the warm mug from my hand. He dumped the green-brown liquid down the drain.

"This stuff isn't FDA approved, and Tia is not going to drink it."

Secretly, I was glad, because the tea smelled like burnt rubber and probably tasted even worse. I whispered words of apology to Gram after I saw how her plump, usually smiling face drooped with disappointment.

Now, as I looked out my bedroom window, I spotted my parents as they stood in a crowd that had grown and moved closer to the dead man. The police had tried to keep everyone back by stringing up yellow police tape, but people were too nosy to keep away completely.

Julius, along with Marco and a few other neighborhood boys, stood and watched the action in silence. But then Marco said something and laughed, like it was an everyday thing to have a dead man at your feet. I held my hand against the glass like it would somehow quiet him. Maybe he would've acted differently if he had seen how the man died.

A policewoman raced toward the boys and towered over Marco's skinny frame. "Y'all show some respect," she said. "Someone has died here."

If I had cared for someone other than myself, maybe he wouldn't have died. With clenched fists, I swept my tears away. But soon enough, there were too many and I couldn't even manage to do that.

Before Marco looked to the ground, he said, "Y–yes, ma'am."

The other boys covered their mouths and tried not to pop with laughter. I wasn't sure if they were laughing at Marco's stutter or just him getting in trouble with the policewoman.

The policewoman, hands on her narrow hips, stared the boys down one by one. That stole away whatever laughter they had left.

Marco's eyes caught on me in my window. He beamed up at me even though there was nothing to be happy about. I pretended not to see him, but after a couple of seconds, when I checked back, he still hadn't looked away.

Julius followed Marco's gaze and when he saw it led to me, he turned to Marco and said something. Marco shrugged, then finally peeled his eyes off me.

As she moved away from the boys, the policewoman spotted me at the window. She stared up at me way longer than necessary, and I shifted uncomfortably. I took a puff of my inhaler, then another. When she began to furiously scribble inside her leather-bound notepad, my heart sped up. I wanted to duck out of the way, but I was stuck in my spot. Did she guess what I had seen?

Awkwardly, I looked away, up to the clear blue sky as if I was wondering if it would rain.

After a painful couple of seconds, the policewoman turned away. I wondered what she'd think of me if she knew what I knew.

# Chapter Three

An unfamiliar man stood in the middle of the crowd that surrounded the dead man. He wore a beige suit and shiny brown shoes, like the kind Principal Wilton wore. A badge of some sort hung from a lanyard around his neck, which told me he was someone important. The sun made his short red hair gleam like the open sign that hung in the corner store window. His skin was pink and splotchy and reminded me of a slice of pizza.

I couldn't hear what the man said, but by the way everyone in the crowd, including my parents, shook their heads or shrugged, I guessed he had asked if they knew anything about the murder. I was glad for the safety of my window.

The policewoman tapped the man's shoulder, and they both moved away from the crowd. I tried my best to read her lips as she spoke, but couldn't.

After a while, the crowd broke up to go about their usual business for a Saturday morning. Some hauled laundry bags. Others pulled grocery carts toward the Shop N Save.

My parents waved to me as they headed for our house. The redheaded man who had been questioning everyone followed their gaze, then turned to the dead man. I figured whatever he was looking for wasn't where I stood, so I relaxed. But when he slowly spun in my direction again, I staggered backward and crashed into my unmade bed.

I paced my bedroom floor. When my parents came in to check on me, Dad hugged me so tightly it scared me.

"What happened?" My voice wobbled.

Dad didn't answer. Instead, he rubbed his head over and over like he was trying to erase something. For the first time, I noticed the stiff little gray hairs that poked out from his short, dark waves.

"Tell me." My hands began to shake. "Please," I said, as I straightened out the bedsheets to give my fingers something to do.

"Alex," Mom said. "We can't protect her forever."

Dad quietly nodded in agreement. "I know."

That was Mom for you. Ever since I was little, her motto had always been that everything's a lesson. When I was in third grade, she had Dad pretend-attack me a dozen ways so I could practice defending myself. Mom had researched techniques on how to escape from a tight grasp or the trunk of a car, and she made me practice them all. Thank goodness Dad drew the line at actually putting me in the trunk of our Honda. Mom wasn't too happy about that, and I had to spend most of that Christmas break watching online escape videos.

I wanted to ask her what kind of a lesson watching someone die was, but I sealed my lips and kept my secret safe.

"Someone was stabbed last night," Mom said.

Dad looked like he needed to go back to bed. He let out

a long sigh and began, "The man in the suit is a detective. He wanted to know if anyone saw . . ." He paused like he was searching for just the right words, but I knew none existed. ". . . who killed the man lying on the sidewalk."

Mom's eyes filled with concern. "We have to be extra careful, Tia. There's a murderer on the loose somewhere in the neighborhood."

At that moment, I almost let it all go. I needed to get the truth far away from me. I wanted to give it to somebody else, to release the dread and worry I felt.

I opened my mouth, but the words wouldn't come out. I took a deep breath, but it only pushed the words further inside. My kneecaps began to shake even though I stood still. They stopped only after I sat cross-legged in the middle of my bed.

Mom sat next to me. "Are you okay?" she said. She was always thinking about how much air I had—or needed. "Dad told me you changed your mind about camp and want to volunteer instead."

I had made up my mind that the only use my new suitcase would get was from my sleepovers at Gram's house. That's when we shared a huge banana split for dinner and watched movies for two days straight. Most times I let Gram pick the movie, which meant we usually watched love stories. Gram had always been a sucker for them, and it wasn't long before I was too.

During these sleepovers, my job was to set up the living room snack tables while Gram popped popcorn in a pot along with a little vegetable oil. One time she added too many kernels and caused the popcorn to burst out of the top and onto the stove. We laughed so hard tears streaked down our cheeks. Popcorn never tasted as good when I made it at home. I loved spending time at Gram's with just the two of us, but I couldn't help feeling brokenhearted.

"Yeah. I'm fine."

"Are you sure? Because I'll need to call and let them know they'll have an extra spot open."

The campers were all chosen by a lottery back in April. I had been one of the lucky ones, and now I was forced to give it all up. I had no other choice.

"I'm sure," I said. "I'll check with the library tomorrow."

"Sounds like a plan," Dad said.

Mom studied me a little longer, and I had trouble keeping the truth inside. Thankfully, Dad distracted her.

"What's wrong with that detective?" Dad said, in a lopsided voice. It reminded me of the warm spots you feel when you're swimming in the ocean. Warm, cold, warm, cold.

He went over to the window but didn't bother to move the sheer curtains aside. "Why would he question everyone out in the open like that? If someone had seen, they'd be too scared to speak up." He continued in a low voice, "And for good reason. The same thing could happen to them in retaliation."

And just like that, Dad confirmed my fear. If anyone found out I was a witness, the killer might come back to hurt me. Or worse, he might go after my family and Julius. That was a risk I could not take.

It was as if I had forgotten how to speak.

On purpose.

_____

That night I could barely sleep. Every time I closed my eyes, I thought up new scenarios about the dead man's family. Maybe he had a daughter the same age I was. Maybe she totally freaked out when she heard somebody took her dad's life like it was up for grabs. She could've even been looking out her window at the same time I had been looking out of mine. Only she had hoped her dad would turn the corner and wave to her. Once home, he'd ask why she was up so late, then kiss her on both temples, the way Dad did to me. But that would never happen for that girl. I knew that hope had died with her dad.

Then I started to think about what my life would've been like if it had been my dad who died on a beautiful summer night, with no one near for comfort except crickets, the moon, and a selfish girl like me.

# Chapter Four

It felt like I had only been asleep for five minutes when late the next morning my cell pinged with a text from *Unknown*. I yawned, then slowly sat up and opened the message. It read: *No one has to know.*

I thought someone had to have typed in the wrong number, and I began to text back to let them know.

*Sorry, but you have* . . .

I looked at the sender again. *Unknown.* Then, I reread the message, and I knew.

The phone tumbled from my loosened fingers. The text hadn't been a mistake. The message was for me and me alone. It was a warning.

I pumped my inhaler while my stomach soared into my chest, then plummeted.

Not only did the killer know where I lived, he had somehow gotten my phone number. As for sending an unknown text, I figured that was easy if you knew where to look online. What else could he do? Hack into my phone camera and watch my every move?

I sprang from bed so quickly that I smacked my hip on the corner of the dresser. I grabbed a shirt from the heap of clothing on the floor and flung it over my phone. Then I rummaged through my desk drawer for something to cover the lens of the camera with. I tossed anything unusable to the floor until I found a small, round adhesive bandage, the kind Dr. Bazaz always applied to the site of a shot. I dropped the bandage twice with my shaky fingers but was finally able to get it into place.

In a way, it felt like the killer had contaminated my phone with his wickedness, so I slathered every inch of it with the blueberry hand sanitizer I kept on my desk. Then I deleted the message and buried the phone inside my sock drawer.

After I got dressed, the doorbell rang.

"Coming," Mom said.

I took two steps at a time, then jumped the last three. I ran toward the front door where Mom stood with her hand almost on the knob. I snatched an umbrella from the coat closet and held it like a baseball bat. I didn't know who stood on our stoop ready to greet us, but I was ready for them.

"Tia?" Mom said as she opened the door. "What in the world are you doing?"

Mom shook her head, then turned toward Julius, who waited outside our door.

I willed the adrenaline away and shoved the umbrella back into the closet. "Um, nothing."

"Good morning, Julius," Mom said, letting him inside.

"You hear what happened?" Julius said to me.

The thin fuzz that had just begun to form over Julius's top lip was as downy as a baby chick. I had the urge to brush it with my fingertips to see if it was as soft as one too.

Cologne wafted into the air as Julius walked past me and into the living room. He never went anywhere without first splashing the woodsy scent onto his neck. After Julius's gram died, Julius's grandpa, Pop-Pop Isaac, had come to live with Julius's family. He filled in for Julius's dad, a plumber, who worked long hours that kept him away from his family, especially in the winter. That's when pipes froze and furnaces broke down from overuse as people tried to beat New York City's long, cold winter.

Pop-Pop Isaac wore cologne every day of his life, and when he died two years ago, Julius took up the tradition.

"Well?" Julius said.

I needed to put as much distance between me and what I had seen as possible. I had to keep my mouth shut, even with Julius, who I had liked since forever and usually told everything to.

I managed a quick nod.

Julius stood close and, for a second, I forgot the man I let die and the anonymous text. I breathed in deeply and tried to extend the forgetting, but it lasted only a second more.

"I can't believe somebody was killed so close to our houses," Julius said.

I felt the truth of what I'd seen tug at me, but I pressed it down and changed the subject.

I took Julius's hand, then opened the front door. "Let's sit out front," I said.

"Wait, shouldn't you be getting ready to leave for camp?"

I swallowed and made room for the lie. "Changed my mind. I'm not going."

Julius jerked his head in surprise. "Really? Why?"

"I decided wasting a whole week of summer vacation at some camp is dumb."

What I couldn't say was that survival camp had already begun and I didn't even have to leave my house.

"But last night you were excited about going."

I stood in the doorway and scanned the block for anyone who might've been watching. As far as I could tell, the coast was clear. "Things change."

He had no idea just how much could change, even overnight.

Just as I was about to tell Mom we were leaving, Gram turned the corner heading toward our house.

Julius rushed down the steps and off the stoop to meet her. He reached for the plain plastic shopping bag she carried. "Let me help you with that," he said.

No identifying marks on the black plastic bag meant Gram had shopped at the botanica again.

"Oh Julius," Gram said, then planted a kiss on his cheek. "You're always so good to me."

That's what I liked most about Julius. He was sweet and thoughtful.

"Have you two had breakfast yet?" Gram said.

"You know I can't function on an empty stomach," Julius said as we followed Gram into the house.

Food had been the last thing on my mind. "I'm not hungry," I said.

Gram plopped down on the couch, causing her skirt to puff out around her. She wore white ankle socks and a pair of silver sandals. Her long ponytail hung over her shoulder and fanned across her chest.

Gram's ponytail was her most prized possession. She brushed her hair every night for an hour while she watched her telenovelas. I thought all the brushing was what made the silver so shiny. Maybe watching soap operas wasn't such the "big waste of time" Dad said it was.

"Where is your suitcase, best granddaughter?"

An unplanned smile escaped. "I'm your only granddaughter."

"Details, details," Gram said. "Shouldn't you be leaving for camp?"

Julius placed the shopping bag down by Gram's feet. "She changed her mind, and I can't say I'm not happy about it. Would've been the most boring week of my life without her here."

Instantly, my face heated up and I couldn't bring myself to look Gram in the eyes.

Julius pointed to the bag. "You buy anything interesting today?"

I sighed. I knew that she always did.

Gram reached inside the bag, then pulled out a tall glass cylinder that contained a red candle. She held it out so we could get a better look.

A skeleton head covered in a white hood gazed back at us. Beneath that, two swords crossed each other.

"Well, that's disturbing," I said.

Julius traced the head with his finger. "Yeah, but in a cool way. What does it say on the back?"

Gram turned it around. "Protection from all evil and harm," she read aloud.

Suddenly, I wasn't so disturbed.

After Gram handed me the candle she said, "Please put this *vela* on the table by the door. I'll light it after I rest."

"How're you going to get Daddy to agree to keep it here?" I said. I hoped Gram had a plan. Suddenly, I really wanted the candle. Anything that promised protection from evil and harm was okay in my book.

"Leave your *papi* to me."

I did what I had been told and put the candle on the table next to the tin box, where we kept our keys.

"Tia, there is something else I wanted to bring here from the botanica, but it was too heavy to carry," Gram said when I got back to the living room. "Will you go and get it for me?"

Julius stood and wiped something invisible from his sneakers. "Sure, we'll get it."

I cut a hard look at Julius. I was happy about the candle but definitely did not want to set foot inside that creepy place.

I slipped my feet into a furry pair of rainbow flip-flops, a birthday gift from Mom. "What is it?" I asked.

"Just tell Celia you're there for me. She's expecting you."

"Tia, wait," Gram said, when we were almost out the door. "Why do you look like that today?"

I smoothed my hair. "Like what?" I said.

She moved my face from side to side. "I can't put my finger on it," she said. "You seem *different*."

"It's my asthma. It kept me awake last night. I'm just tired," I said confidently, since I told the truth, just not the whole truth.

"Okay," Gram said. "You two be careful out there."

Gram's eyes lingered on my face a little longer, but then we were on our way.

Usually, I wanted to buy the things we needed from the places ordinary people bought their stuff from. But maybe the botanica had more than a creepy candle to offer for protection? If it did, I wanted it. I needed all the protection I could get.

# Chapter Five

On the ground in front of my house, words written in yellow chalk greeted me like a punch to the face.

"Who wrote this?"

The words exploded from me and startled two of my neighbor's daughters, Aiva and Juliet, who were playing outside their house two houses away. They looked hesitantly at each other before they scrambled over to see what the fuss was about.

"Well?" I demanded, hoping they'd confess to it.

Aiva studied the words. "Not me," she said.

"Me neither," Juliet said.

"Of course you didn't," Aiva said. "You don't even know how to read."

Juliet stomped her foot. "I do too. It says, 'I . . . know you . . . saw me . . . looking at you.'"

"Good job," Aiva said.

"Told you," Juliet said. Then they skipped back to their house, where they happily resumed whatever game they had been playing.

The words seemed to vibrate against the concrete. Another reminder to keep my mouth shut. I steadied myself against the fire hydrant to keep from going down.

Julius reached for my arm. "Whoa, you okay?"

I nodded.

I didn't know how long the words had been there, but I searched the area all the same. And just like earlier when I first scanned the block for any shady characters, there was no one.

I sat doubled over on the first step. Sweat rolled sluggishly behind my ears and onto my neck. The sweltering summer air grew thick, and soon I felt like I had been caught up in a rip current, struggling to make my way back to land.

Julius eyed me suspiciously, then rubbed at the yellow words with his foot. "It's only chalk," he said. "No biggie."

Just then, Emelia and Big Mike strolled by. Emelia, who wore her signature black T-shirt and high-waisted jeans, had her hand stuffed inside Big Mike's back pocket. Mike was a senior in high school and had a full-on goatee that made him look evil, which wasn't too far from the truth. Big Mike's shady behavior got the attention of the outside world when he was fifteen. Before that, only kids at school and in the neighborhood knew what Mike was really like. At school, he tripped kids on the staircase just to see how far they'd stumble before hitting the floor. It had been his entertainment. He called it "Bowling for Nerds." Big Mike used to bust in and take photos of people while they used the bathroom, which he then texted to everyone. He went for broke one Monday morning when he slammed a substitute teacher against a wall of lockers after he was caught setting fire to a mop in the janitor's closet. I didn't know all the details, but I did know he went straight to juvie soon after. You could almost hear a collective sigh of relief throughout the entire school.

Mr. Booth, Emelia's dad, had custody of her and her brother ever since their mom ran away with the neighborhood podiatrist just a few months after her bunion surgery. People used to crack jokes about that, but that was when it was fresh gossip. As time went on, it became just another story woven into our Brooklyn neighborhood's history.

I watched Big Mike and Emelia and wondered how her dad allowed her to hang out with him. Not that it mattered. Emelia wasn't exactly a rule follower. I never bought into the excuse that "she was the way she was because her mom abandoned her," blah, blah, blah. I believed she'd be the same person, with or without her mom.

Julius stepped back from Big Mike. "Yeah," Big Mike said, "that's right. Move aside, move aside." He draped his arm across Emelia's bony shoulders. "Maybe that dead dude didn't give somebody enough room and that's why they offed him."

"You shouldn't make fun of dead people," I said.

"Oh yeah, why do you care so much? He your relative or something?"

Julius pulled me to my feet. "C'mon, T, we have to g–go," he said.

"Yeah," Mike said, "you have to go–go."

I wanted so badly to come to Julius's defense, but my mind was stuck on the yellow words across the pavement.

"Let's go," Julius said and led me toward the botanica.

Big Mike's and Emelia's laughter followed us even after we turned the corner.

Julius dragged me along and, before I knew it, I began to wheeze. "Wait," I shook my inhaler.

"Believe me when I tell you, Tia, you don't want to mess around with Big Mike."

I was relieved he didn't want to talk about how weird I was about the chalk message.

"Why?" I said. "He's the same jerk he's always been."

Julius leaned in and whispered so softly that I had to watch his lips to understand what he said. The scent of his coconut lip balm drew me in even closer.

"Because I think maybe Big Mike is the one who killed that guy," he said.

I didn't want to let Julius go on believing it was Big Mike. He was wrong, that I knew for sure. But I couldn't really correct him without telling my secret.

Julius watched as I sucked down my medicine. "Well?" he said when I was done.

"Who knows?" was all I could muster. As Dad would say, my answer was "neither here nor there." But seemed to be good enough for Julius, because he didn't question me.

We took a shortcut through the parking lot behind Bubbles, our neighborhood laundromat, and made it to the cherry factory in five minutes. From there, the botanica was another four blocks away.

It was break time and some of the factory workers, with their bright-red hands and cups of iced coffee, sat on the sidewalk with their backs against the brick building. Their stained fingers made them all look like murderers.

I knew a couple of the workers because Dad worked there as supervisor, but he wasn't with the others today. He had probably gone home for a quick cup of Mom's special coffee. A cup of Mom's coffee in the early afternoon was what Dad called a "perk." That, and the fact that the factory was only four blocks from home.

I had a perk of my own and that was the fact that we always had an industrial-sized jar of cherries in our fridge. They were the sweet kind you'd buy at the grocery store especially for ice cream sundaes.

"Hey, Tia," Mr. Hernandez said as we walked by.

Mr. Hernandez and Dad had never gotten along. Mr. Hernandez was mad when Dad got promoted to supervisor even though Mr. Hernandez had been working there longer. He had given Dad a hard time ever since.

Once, money went missing from a collection they had taken up for a sick coworker. Dad thought Mr. Hernandez was responsible since he was the last one seen with the envelope of money. Things had also gone missing from the employee lockers. Dad thought Mr. Hernandez might have been responsible for that too. Dad said the second he had solid proof he would go to management with it.

"Hi," I mumbled. I felt weird talking to Dad's archenemy.

After he took a long drink of his Diet Coke, Mr. Hernandez said, "Hey, Williams, is it true the guy was stabbed?" Plenty loud enough for Julius and me to hear.

"That's what I heard," said another man.

I nervously tightened my ponytail even though it hadn't come loose.

Julius gave me a look that said "let's go," and we began to slowly inch away. Most times a conversation with adults was awkward like that. You just never knew when, or how, to make an exit and I was glad for Julius's hint.

Just then, a whistle sounded inside the factory, letting everyone know break time was over. It reminded me of the signal school used to let us know when it was time to change classes.

"Tia, you and your friend be cautious out here, okay?" Mr. Harper, the man in charge of loading the delivery trucks, called after us. Dad had said he was one of the nicest people at the factory. "Terrible things can happen in broad daylight, too, not just in the middle of the night."

I usually felt safer in the daylight, but all that changed with this morning's warnings. Mr. Harper was right. We had to be careful.

"We will," Julius said.

When we were out of earshot, I asked why Julius thought Big Mike was the killer.

"Didn't you see those red drops on his sneakers?"

I hadn't noticed, but it didn't matter. The killer was shorter than Big Mike, but I couldn't tell Julius that.

"No, you're the only one in the world who checks to see who's wearing the cleanest sneakers," I said.

"Very funny. Those drops could've been blood."

"Maybe he had a bloody nose, or a really bad paper cut," I said.

Julius kept talking like I hadn't said anything. "I'm going to tell the cops. The detective said we should call him if we knew something."

I realized whatever I said would come out sounding suspicious, but I couldn't help myself.

"Julius, please, just mind your own business."

"What? Why?" Julius said, hurt.

"Because," I started, "my father said the same thing could happen to anyone who speaks up."

The next thing I knew, I was stumbling on a lopsided section of sidewalk. In a split second, I hit the ground on the most deserted block in our neighborhood. No houses, no stores, no people. Just a car dealership that had gone out of business two years before.

Julius knelt beside me. "T! Are you okay?"

I reached for my inhaler. "Yeah," I wheezed, rubbing my knee. "I'm fine, nothing broken or bleeding."

I pumped, then held the medicine deep inside my lungs until I felt lightheaded.

After a minute Julius said, "Look!"

I followed where his eyes led. Red, dime-sized dots littered the pavement. "What? It's just cherry juice."

"This couldn't be from the cherry factory," Julius said. "Not this far away."

I scrambled to my feet like whatever was on the sidewalk could somehow attach itself to me. "We're not that far, Julius,"

I said, trying to convince myself. "Come on. Gram will start wondering where we are soon."

Then Julius said what I tried not to think about. "No way, I think it's blood."

For someone who used to be squeamish around blood, Julius did a thorough job as he inspected the drops.

"That's it, I'm calling the police," Julius said. His forehead almost touched the pavement. "This could help find whoever killed that man."

"Can't we talk about something other than that stupid dead guy?" I said.

Julius flinched at the word *stupid*, and I didn't blame him.

"What's your problem, T?" Julius said.

"I don't have a problem!" I felt like a little kid who'd gone into tantrum mode, but I didn't care. I meant it. I was tired of talking about the dead guy, but most of all I was tired of thinking about him.

I sprinted off. If I couldn't unsee what I'd seen that night, then the only thing that was important to me right now was to find whatever protection the botanica had to offer. Even if it made me a hypocrite.

# Chapter Six

The botanica was stuffed between a dollar store and a small grocery store with a sign on the door that announced shoplifters would be prosecuted. Someone had written on the sign with black magic marker and turned *prosecuted* into *executed*. If it were any other day, I would've had a good laugh over that, but nothing made me crack even the smallest of smiles.

A wooden sign hung from the brick front just over the botanica's door. It featured one huge blue eye and read *Botanica Mystical Shop*. A breeze kicked up and the sign squeaked softly in response.

As I waited for Julius to catch up, a man watched me from across the street. He was partially hidden in the shadow of a large tree, but I could tell he was smiling. I glanced behind me thinking he had to be looking at someone else nearby, but I was alone. When I turned toward him again, his smile had vanished, and he began to walk in my direction.

The lower half of my body felt tingly and hot. Maybe my brain had sent extra energy to my legs knowing I'd need it to get away in a hurry. I sprinted for the door of the botanica. Just as Julius reached me, the man changed course and jogged away.

"Why did you take off like that?" Julius said.

I watched the man until he was out of sight.

"Well?"

"Oh, just felt like running," I said. "That's all."

"Stop lying, T. Something's wrong, and I want to know what."

Blood still pounded its way through my body. My heartbeat thumped inside my ears and heat stirred within my chest. It was almost like the dead man's ghost called out to me, begging. *Tell, tell, TELL*. The words crashed against my skull, over and over.

"Okay," I said, startling Julius almost as much as myself. "I saw—"

Just then, the door to the botanica swung open and set off a small bell fastened to the top of the door. A frazzled mom and her three kids stumbled out onto the sidewalk. The littlest boy gave me a toothless smile.

"What did you see?" Julius said.

But I had chickened out. "Never mind," I said.

Julius eyeballed me, demanding I tell him.

I shook out my sweaty hands. "Forget it, it's nothing," I said, then slipped inside the shop.

Dad would've killed me if he knew I went to the botanica. He thought the store was full of witches and spells. Gram insisted that wasn't true. She said it was filled with goodness and inspiration and that, sometimes, God needed a little nudging in the direction you wanted things to go. Either way, if the botanica offered some sort of spell, inspiration, or prodding that could help me, then I wanted it. I needed my life to get back to what it used to be—who I used to be. I didn't care where it came from, as long as it worked.

The botanica was smaller than I had imagined. About half a dozen people browsed the store, but the only murmurs took place behind a red velvet curtain near the cash register.

A wobbly ceiling fan above the cash register spun slowly in a sluggish beat.

Directly in front of us stood a long wooden cabinet. It was tall and held at least fifty small drawers. Each one had a small brown metal hook instead of a knob. Whatever shine the cabinet once had was worn off, especially around the hooks.

When I got closer, I saw each drawer had a label that identified its contents. No matter how hard I squinted, the tiny script was impossible to read. I ran my fingers along the smooth wood and wondered what those tiny drawers could possibly hold. On top of the cabinet, smack in the middle, sat an enormous container. It looked like the old water jug Dad brought home from work. We'd used it to save up change, and when it reached a certain point, we brought it all to the bank where we used a coin-counting machine. One time we had over eight hundred dollars. We used it to buy Gram a new couch.

But this jug was filled with green liquid. Floating inside were brown pieces of what looked to me like cut-up earthworms, the kind that came out of nowhere after a heavy rainstorm. The ones Julius rescued when they ended up in a place where they could've gotten squished. I once asked him what they felt like, and his answer was to chase me with one. It had swayed back and forth as Julius held it out toward me. Poor thing was probably more afraid than I was.

A small card taped to the bottom of the jug explained the concoction was used to attract money. I was glad Gram never came home with something that gross. Dad wouldn't have been the only one who had a problem with it.

To the right of the entrance, a glass case situated along the wall showed off small brown bottles, angel statues, candles, boxes of "cleansing" oils, and different types of tarot cards. Plastic spinning racks held beaded necklaces in assorted colors and shapes, odd bracelets featuring eyeballs, and medals with faces of saints imprinted on them.

"A third eye would come in handy," Julius said, then held a bracelet to the middle of his forehead. "Then I wouldn't miss a thing."

I took it from him and placed it back on the rack.

I spotted Saint María Goretti, the patron saint of girls and teenagers, two rows away. When I turned thirteen, Gram had given me the same medal. I hadn't been surprised because she'd given Mom Saint Apollonia, the patron saint of toothaches, when Mom had a root canal. Mom's saint wore a necklace with a gold-colored tooth hanging from it. I thought it was gross and was glad not to be the one with a toothache. Gram explained that almost every profession has a saint dedicated to it. Even librarians have Saint Jerome.

"Why in the world would a librarian ever need protection?" I'd asked her. "Will the books rebel one day?"

I cracked myself up but stopped giggling when I saw Gram's serious face. "Books will always need to be safeguarded."

At first, I thought she exaggerated, but then I thought about how Mrs. Cantor, the PTA president at our neighborhood's only private school, tried to ban two books and I realized Gram had been right. Luckily, the principal didn't agree, and Mrs. Cantor quit. I'd wondered if the principal knew about Saint Jerome.

I spun the rack three times and hoped there'd be a medal and a saint dedicated to protection. I had ten dollars leftover from my birthday money, and it burned a hole inside my pocket, but no luck. I still held out hope though. I had the whole rest of the place to explore.

Every time the front door opened, I expected to see the man who had watched me from the shadows. I wondered if the store's workers could somehow detect if a murderer entered.

A long table took up most of the back of the store. The fancy white tablecloth reminded me of the one we used for Thanksgiving and Christmas Eve. The bottom of it fluttered gently in the slight breeze of the air conditioner.

White curtains hung from a rod on the ceiling, just above the table. Thick red tassels held each one open as though it invited us to take a closer look.

High on the wall behind the table hung the biggest crucifix I'd ever seen outside of church. Assembled on wooden shelves made to look like a staircase sat angel figurines, lit candles, and burning incense. Tall glass vases filled with red and white flowers stood on the floor at either side of the table.

A man dressed in a white suit stepped out from behind a door next to the table. At least four of the beaded necklaces like I had seen earlier hung from his neck. His dark hair was slicked back with so much gel, it seemed like LEGO man hair. His hairline showed off what Gram called "a widow's peak."

The man stood by the door and never took his eyes off us. I did my best to ignore him, but under his steady gaze I started to feel like a thief.

I strolled slowly around the store and carefully checked out the other merchandise. Julius stuck close behind.

"What're you doing?" he said. "Go ask that guy about Gram's stuff."

"We have to talk to Celia, and he's obviously not her. Besides, I want to look around."

I searched a wall of necklaces, but without tags written in English, it was a waste of time. I understood some of the things Gram said to me in Spanish, but I couldn't read or speak it.

There was plenty to see inside the lighted case where I stood, so I bent down to get a better look. The other side of it was mirrored, and I could see Julius's feet behind me. I also saw that my hair was a wreck. The neat ponytail I had left my house with was gone, and in its place was a halo of chaotic frizz. It seemed like my hair had been hit with Miracle-Gro. I loved summer, but New York's humidity had always hated my curly hair. I slid the hairband out, then tried to tame my wiry strands, but it didn't help at all.

And, like most everything else in the store, many of the candle labels in the case were written in Spanish.

In the mirror, Julius's feet marched weirdly like he had to pee.

"Cut it out," I hissed.

"What?"

I used one hand to steady myself against the case, then spun around on my heel. I didn't know why the marching bothered me, but it did. "The foot thing."

Julius joined me down on one knee. "Stop worrying about my feet. Let's get Gram's stuff and go," he said. "That guy in white is creeping me out. He hasn't taken his big, googly eyes off us the whole time we've been here."

I turned my attention back to the candles.

"And what's up with his hair?" Julius added.

White pants suddenly appeared in the mirror. I didn't have to turn around to know who they belonged to. I elbowed Julius, but he didn't get the hint and kept right on talking.

"It looks like there's a sick black dog stretched across his head," he finished with a snicker.

"A sick *perro*," the man said, "would be a very, very sad thing, *muchacho*, eh?"

Julius stood so fast he bumped into my shoulder and caused me to lose my balance. I landed squarely on top of LEGO Man's shiny white shoes.

I struggled to my feet. "Oh, I'm sorry!" I said.

"I didn't mean anything by . . . ," Julius said, embarrassed.

"Is there something here I can help you two with?" the man said.

"I have to pick up something for my grandmother," I said.

"And who is your grandmother?"

"Frances Lugo."

The man's eyebrows shot toward his creased forehead. "Your *abuela* is Frances?" he said.

"Yeah," Julius said.

"Yours too?" the man asked.

"Oh no, not mine." Julius poked me hard with his finger. "Hers."

"Oww," I whispered. "We're supposed to ask for Celia."

"Celia?" the man said. "Are you sure?"

"Yes, that's what she—I mean, my grandmother—told us."

"You two stay right here. I'll find her for you."

The man walked away, then stopped and said something in Spanish to one of the employees. She looked at us and smiled.

"What's that all about?" Julius said. His lips barely moved, like a ventriloquist's.

"I've no idea."

The man continued behind the curtain near the register. After a couple of minutes, he returned with a short, bowlegged woman dressed in all white, from the bandana fastened around her head with the knot tied in front, to knee-high socks rolled down to her ankles, exposing the boniest legs I'd ever seen. The woman, who was older than Gram, held a fat cigar between her wrinkled, crooked fingers. Her crinkly brown skin looked like it had always been that way. The lines were deep and reminded me of photos I'd seen in my social studies textbook of dried-up riverbeds.

"So," the old woman said, "you're Frances's granddaughter?"

"Yes," I said.

She nodded slowly. The old woman squinted like she had a hard time focusing. "I'm Celia."

Celia moved closer, then placed the lit cigar between her thin, dry lips and puffed. A million tiny lines appeared and seemed to grab hold of the cigar. I tried to take a step back, but Julius stood directly behind me, leaving no room.

Cigar smoke soon caused me to cough. Nervously, I checked my pocket for my inhaler.

After she sucked on the glowing cigar for what seemed like an hour, Celia spoke. "There's something I don't understand yet, but it's in your eyes. *Sí, sí*"—her words rode the smoke—"you need a *limpia*."

I had heard that word before but couldn't remember what it meant. LEGO Man pulled open the curtain, then stood stiff and formal as if awaiting a queen. "Enter," he said.

"No, thank you," Julius replied, "we're not hungry."

Celia chuckled.

"A *limpia* isn't food," LEGO Man said impatiently. "It's a spiritual cleansing."

Julius opened his mouth and I was afraid he'd tell them he had already showered, but I knew about cleansings from Gram. Some people believed if they were cleansed, it would eliminate negative energy or chase away bad spirits. Others went to be cleansed to rid themselves of an addiction, or to remove bad luck from their lives. Some said that being cleansed could even bring peace and understanding to someone who was confused or fearful. I fit into the latter but had no idea how Celia could known that. I wondered if Dad had been right the whole time. Maybe the botanica truly was filled with witches.

Celia placed her raisin-like hand on my arm. It felt exactly how it looked—dry and warm. "*Vámonos*," she said.

I didn't know if Celia could help me, but I had to give it a try. "Okay," I said.

I allowed myself to be guided toward the curtain.

Julius followed closely behind, but LEGO Man stopped him at the curtain. "I'm going in, too!" Julius said.

LEGO Man adjusted the cuffs of his suit jacket. "No," he said. "You have to wait here."

"What?" Julius said, loud and high-pitched. "Why?"

"That's the rule."

"No way, Tia," Julius said. "This is too weird. Let's get out of here."

I hesitated and wondered if going behind the curtain with Celia would make me a witch too.

Celia made up my mind for me and pushed me through. LEGO Man closed the curtain behind us.

# Chapter Seven

I worried I had made a huge mistake. The room was warm, and the air felt heavy. The dark purple walls, lit only by candles set up on a round table, didn't help things. Shadows flickered and swayed across the room in a slow dance.

Next to the candles, three tall, clear glasses filled with what looked like water stood side by side. A statue of Jesus, arms opened wide in a welcoming stance, commanded attention from the middle of the table. I relaxed a little and thought that if Jesus was there, maybe it was okay for me to be there too.

Two identical large chairs positioned at the back of the room looked uncomfortable, with straight backs and hardly any cushioning.

In the corner, near the chairs, two sculptures sat on a shelf. One was of a man who wore a crown adorned with jewels and who held a golden staff, and the other, an angel, held a sword and shield. Before each statue lay a small, round saucer, like the ones Gram used with her teacups.

Celia quietly slid a wheeled, black-leather office chair to where I stood. "*Siéntate*," she said.

Gram had said that word a million times. Celia wanted me

to sit, but I wasn't crazy about the idea in case I had to make a run for it. "No, thank you," I said. "I'll stand."

After she placed the glowing end of her cigar in one of the saucers, Celia thrust me into the chair.

Not knowing what to expect next, I covered my face using both hands. "Don't!"

"Do not be afraid," Celia soothed.

It was hard not to be after the thrusting, but I managed a shaky nod and watched as she pulled out a white wicker basket from underneath a nearby table. In it, a bunch of green, weedy plants tied together with twine lay at the bottom.

"For your *abuela* I do this," the old woman said as she placed the plants over my head. I thought she was going to slap me with them, so I ducked. She laughed, showing off a smile minus a couple of teeth. "And for you," she finished.

I glanced at Jesus, then closed my eyes and prayed that he'd listen to the silent plea I needed him to hear. The nudge I tried hard to give. I closed my eyes to keep the pooling tears hidden.

A swooshing sound began above my head, then a small breeze. Celia used the plants to fan me, then suddenly she cupped my shoulder and began to spin my chair. I thought it might be better for my eyes if they rested while Celia worked, so I kept them tightly closed.

Celia started to hum a slow, unhappy tune. It reminded me of a scary movie Julius and I watched when we were little. It had been about a doll who came to life every night.

After a couple of minutes, Celia's humming changed its

slow tempo to a short and demanding rhythm, almost like angry, wordless sentences. My heart danced wildly in time.

The spinning slowed to a stop, and that's when the words finally came. They were more like a lullaby, soft and calming, but I didn't recognize any of them. For the first time in my life, I was mad at myself for never completely learning Spanish.

The sound of trickling liquid reached my ears as Celia rambled on. I peeked to see what was going on.

"*Cierra los ojos,*" Celia scolded.

Thankfully, another word I knew. Gram had always reminded me to close the refrigerator. *Cerrado*, she'd say, tapping on the door.

Next, a wet finger touched each of my eyelids.

Celia slowly began to circle my chair and repeated the words in an unfamiliar voice. Every muscle in my body tightened as I waited for whatever would happen next. Her voice was raspier than before. The worn-out wooden floor creaked with each step she took. As she went, she blew cigar smoke all around me. The staleness of it gagged me until I ducked my nose into my shirt. It was still bad, but at least it had been diluted by the scent of my Ooh-La-La Lavender deodorant.

"*Descansa los ojos,*" Celia said.

I pieced the words together. A couple I knew, but the rest I got from Gram's telenovelas. The old woman wished my eyes peace. Two thoughts collided in confusion. The first was that I knew for sure this small, wrinkled, cigar-smoking lady was a witch. The second was that I wanted to tell Dad he'd been right all these years. Witches did exist, and they existed in the botanica. But I knew there was no way I could ever tell him, not without being put under house arrest for the remainder of the summer, or maybe even longer. I decided to just be happy with knowing that a spell—or whatever had gone on—had been placed on me without me even having to ask for it.

"*Hecho*," Celia said. "It is done. Open your eyes."

At first, I was afraid to. I wanted to wait a few extra minutes to make sure the spell had enough time to settle over me, but the old woman insisted.

She pried open my eyelids. "*Abre los ojos*," she said.

I had to blink a few times before I could focus. My eyelids felt sticky and my eyes burned a little.

Celia smiled big. "You look just like your father when he was a boy," she said. Then she pointed to my eyes. "Same beautiful *ojos*."

"I know your *abuelita* is very proud of you." She gave my hands a squeeze. "She talks about you all the time when she comes," Celia said.

Every inch of me sagged beneath her words. If Gram ever found out about my secret, she'd probably be ashamed of me for the rest of her life.

Celia stood and inhaled deeply. "It is time for you to go. Whatever was troubling you will be better now."

I followed Celia to the opening in the curtain and wondered how long the spell would take to work, because at that moment, I felt as vulnerable as when I walked in.

Celia pointed to the huge angel statue on the shelf. "Don't forget what you came for," she said.

"That's Gram's?" I said. "Why in the world does she want that?"

"Archangel Michael is the most powerful and greatest spiritual protector," Celia said, stunned. "Your house will need him, so place him near your front door. You will also need these." She held up three beaded necklaces and a small brown bottle from the basket on the floor.

Celia reached for one of those telltale bags. "I don't need that," I said.

"All right," she said and placed the necklaces around my neck.

Each set of beads was a different color. Blue, white, and purple.

"What I'm about to say to you is *importante*," Celia said. "You must bathe in this oil." She pointed to the bottle, then handed it to me.

Celia closed her eyes and swayed away from me. When I reached out to steady her, she touched each necklace as if nothing had happened. "The purple beads represent strength, the blue beads, truth, and the white beads, higher power."

I nodded, then tucked the necklaces into my shirt and the little bottle into the pocket of my shorts.

"Thank you," I said, ready to leave the stuffy room.

Celia tugged on my arm. "And remember," she said, her eyes narrowed, "to lie still. As still as a dead . . . *gato*."

I didn't think things could have possibly gotten any weirder. A dead cat? I wasn't sure I had translated the word correctly, so I chose to ignore it.

# Chapter Eight

The store seemed much cooler and brighter now than when I went behind the curtain.

Julius hurried over. "Are you okay?" he said.

"Yeah, I'm fine. It was no big deal. She gave me Gram's angel statue, that's all," I lied.

"Doesn't matter, you should've never gone back there alone," he said. He took hold of the statue. "While you were gone, that dude in the funky white suit tried to get me to buy some stupid love potion."

"Love potion?" I said, happy to talk about something else. "Did you buy it?"

For a few silent seconds, Julius stared at me. "You know I don't need a potion," he said finally.

"Oh, I'm . . . I mean that's . . . ," I looked down at my feet. "You know, good." *Good* came out sounding like "glood," but Julius didn't seem to notice.

"Let's get out of here," he said. "The old lady and that guy are freaks."

"They're not," I mumbled.

"How do you know? They're not going to say, 'Hi, I'm

a freak.' That's why freaks get away with stuff. Freaks stay undercover."

"Well, Celia isn't a freak," I said. I left out the part about her being a witch.

"Really?" Julius said. "So, you like this place now?"

"No! I'm just saying they weren't so bad."

Julius wrestled with the statue and tried to get a better grip. "Didn't they give you a bag or something we can carry this thing in?"

I felt bad for Julius's struggle. I shook my head.

The bell above the door broadcasted our exit.

LEGO Man made his way to us. "Celia said to follow her directions exactly as she has instructed." I nodded slightly and hoped Julius hadn't paid attention, then quickly exited.

After I scanned the block for anyone who looked iffy or like a murderer, I spotted a family walking toward the Catholic church across the street. A large cross reached high into the sky from the pointed roof. The rough gray stones of the outside walls glistened in the sunlight like they were covered in millions of pin-sized diamonds.

Three little girls held hands and quickly skipped up the church steps. Their neatly braided hair bounced in unison. Their mom held a tiny bundle in her arms as she carefully stepped around a tree root that jutted up through the broken sidewalk.

"Girls," a man said as he adjusted the blue diaper bag that dangled from his shoulder. "Wait for us, please."

I wondered what it felt like to be part of a family that big.

To have siblings to play with and confide in. If I had an older sister or brother, I would've confessed to them what I saw, and together we'd be able to keep our family safe.

I watched the girls with envy and hoped they knew how lucky they were.

The church's large wooden doors were out of place on the crowded Brooklyn street. They seemed as if they belonged to a castle in England instead.

Massive and thick, the doors squealed in defiance when the giggling girls heaved them open.

The family disappeared into the coolness of the church and left nothing behind but my ache to have a sibling.

As soon as we reached the corner, a loud *CRACK!* broke through the low whir of city noise.

"Oh no!" I said from a crouched position. "Get down, Jul!"

Julius looked around but didn't make a move. Instead, he gawked at me like I had lost my mind. "It's okay. Those guys are working. That's all."

The moment he said it, I knew he was right. Just behind Julius, two city workers wearing bright-orange vests stood in the middle of the street. They had just dropped a manhole cover into place.

I got to my feet without another word. I couldn't explain that I thought the murderer had found us.

My legs were still jelly when Julius rested the statue on a mailbox a block later. He steadied it with one hand. "Okay," he said. "What was that all about back there?"

"Um, the noise scared me, that's all," I said.

"You expect me to believe that? You looked like you were in enemy territory or something."

That was the thing—I had no idea where or when the enemy would show up, so the whole world was a potential danger zone.

"Well?" Julius said.

"It's the truth. I got scared. I mean, that thing is like a thousand pounds." It felt good to tell the truth, and I had even managed a grin.

Julius studied me a minute longer, then said, "So, what did Mr. Freaky in the white suit mean by 'instructions'?"

"Oh, it was just about that," I said, then pointed to the statue. "Gram's supposed to place it by the front door."

I was back to telling only part truths again, but Julius seemed satisfied with the explanation. A small part of me worried about how easy omitting the truth was becoming, but I had to do what I had to do.

"Come on," Julius said. "We'd better get home. This sucker is heavy."

When we got to the old car dealership, someone yelled out from behind us, "Hey, what're you kids doing here?"

It was Mr. Hernandez. When we'd first seen him, he'd been wearing a blue long-sleeved uniform shirt rolled up past his elbows. Now, he wore a white sleeveless T-shirt, the kind Dad wore underneath his button-down shirts. It exposed a poorly written tattoo across his left bicep. His plump stomach hung below his belt. Part of his uniform shirt had been tucked into his back pocket. The rest of it hung down like a tail.

The weeds rustled in the breeze like a giant had reached down and run his fingers through them. Other than that, there were no sounds. No car horns. No kids playing in the summer sun. No people strolling by with their dogs.

We were alone.

# Chapter Nine

Slowly, Mr. Hernandez removed a cigarette from its pack. "I'm on my way to . . . um, a doctor's appointment, but first I need a smoke. You got a light?"

"No!" Julius answered, like a shot. "I mean, we don't smoke."

The phlegm in Mr. Hernandez's chest rattled with laughter. "Of course you don't." The laugh ended suddenly and unfinished. "You two shouldn't be roaming around the neighborhood alone. Especially around here."

"You're right," Julius said. "We were just leaving now anyway. Come on, Tia."

"It means 'what worries you, masters you,'" Mr. Hernandez said. He'd caught me trying to make out the overdone curly font of his tattoo.

I wondered if the dead guy had any tattoos and what they might have been. Maybe he had his daughter's name etched into his skin so that she'd always be close. Or maybe it was his mother he needed to be close to. That made me think of my own mom, and I had to swallow extra hard to gulp down the golf ball that had suddenly materialized inside my throat.

Mr. Hernandez patted the tattoo. "It's why I never worry. I have no masters. What about you? You got any worries?"

His questions swirled around me like a hurricane had kicked up without warning, and for a minute, everything around us faded away. It was just me, Mr. Hernandez, and the spotted sidewalk. It was like a scene in a TV show where everything got quiet and the camera zoomed in on one person's face. I was that person.

Maybe he somehow knew what I saw, and if he did, he'd blab it to the whole neighborhood. Word would eventually make it back to the killer, and just like a changing tale in a game of telephone, he'd think I had been the one who'd done the telling.

I allowed the details of that night to play inside my head. Not even a city bus had passed, and they ran all through the night. It seemed impossible that Mr. Hernandez would know anything. Still, I worried.

It was Julius who broke the spell. "Nah, we're too young for worrying. We leave that to the adults, right, Tia?"

My hands balled tightly into fists and left tiny horseshoe shapes imprinted on my damp palms. How I wished that were true. "Right, no worrying here," I said.

Mr. Hernandez's chest vibrated again as he continued in the opposite direction. "Don't be so serious," he said. Then just as he turned the corner, he added, "Life's too short, you know?"

Chills swept across my body. "Wait, what do you—"

"Who cares what he means, T? Let him go," Julius said. "He's freaking weird. Maybe it wasn't Big Mike. Maybe it was Hernandez."

I thought about how Mr. Hernandez was much heavier than the killer. "Doubt it," I said.

"Could be, you know. Murderers don't exactly go around wearing signs that say, 'Hey, watch your back because I just might sink a knife into it.' Everyone is a suspect in my book."

When we had gotten a block away from home, we ran into Danielle Nevins and Tiny Reed, who were hanging outside Tiny's house. If you believed that opposites attract, that would explain their friendship. Danielle was taller and bigger than anyone in our school. In PE, no one ever wanted to play dodgeball or any contact sport opposite her. I'd even seen some people run away, not caring about lost points or total defeat. I was lucky not to have to take part in PE. At least my asthma had been good for something.

Tiny is just that. She was born prematurely, and some people said her mother died of some rare disease right after she was born. Others said Tiny was left on a bench at the B61 bus stop on Atlantic Avenue. Nobody knew for sure what the truth was. There was only one fact, and that was that Tiny had been raised by parents who treated her like a princess. They bought her whatever she asked for. She always had the latest gadgets and the best sneakers. I'd never been inside her house, but I'd heard it was like walking right into one of those expensive architect magazines on bookstore shelves.

Tiny and Danielle had been friends since the third grade, when Victoria Jackson rammed into Tiny during lunch period, then chuckled as Tiny slid across the floor riding a mound of smashed peas. It looked like somebody had used a slingshot to catapult Tiny at least five feet across the grimy cafeteria floor.

Danielle had stood up from her lunch table and demanded to know who the culprit was. The whole room fell silent. Then everybody, me included, pointed to Victoria like a compass needle points to the North Pole. It didn't take but a few seconds for Victoria to stammer out an apology and then lie about how it was an accident. Danielle made it over to Victoria in no time at all but was only able to hover over her for a second before the lunch aides interrupted. That was all it took though, because the point had been made. Don't ever mess with Tiny. Suddenly, Tiny became everyone's good friend.

Tiny shoved playfully into Danielle, who didn't budge. "No, she didn't! Stop lying," she said.

Danielle looked insulted. "You know I don't lie," she said.

Tiny adjusted the buckle of her mint-green sandals. "Wow, then she's really stupid."

"And crazy!" Danielle added. "The internet isn't a darn diary. The whole world will have access to that stuff!"

It was obvious they weren't going to move for us, and when we maneuvered around them, I tripped over Danielle's huge feet. Thankfully, I caught myself before I fell and made a complete idiot of myself.

"Hey—" Danielle stopped mid-yelp when she spotted Julius. "Oh, hey, Julius," she said, then sniffed the air.

Julius placed the statue at his feet. "What's up, D. Who's stupid?" he said.

Danielle shielded her eyes from the sun and smiled at him.

I hated to admit it, but Danielle was pretty, and the way she ogled Julius really bothered me. I don't know how, but her brown eyes seemed to shine more than ordinary ones like mine. Her skin was clear and her teeth straight and bright white. It felt so unfair that at least once a week I have to smear on this smelly pimple cream that Gram concocted from ingredients she bought at the botanica.

"Is that you who's smelling so . . . divine?" Danielle said.

*Divine?* I almost choked on the old-timey word.

Julius ran his hand across his glossy hair. "Yeah, you know, I was born smelling good."

"Are you for real?" I said.

Julius smiled big and goofy and looked adorable.

"I believe it," Danielle said, in a hypnotic daze.

"Pfft, I don't," Tiny said.

Tiny gave me a once-over. "I thought you were going to that stupid camp thing this summer," she said. "Didn't it start today?"

The day I found out I had been selected, Tiny overheard me as I squealed about it to Julius. Now I was sorry I had ever filled out the application, and even sorrier that I got in.

"Yeah, but I changed my mind about going," I said.

Tiny stared at me open-mouthed before she found her voice. "You took up a spot and didn't use it?"

"Well—"

"Well nothing!"

"Wait," Danielle said. "Tiny, isn't that the camp you didn't get into?"

Tiny laughed half-heartedly. "Are you crazy? You wouldn't catch me going to some stupid survival camp."

With a hand on her hip, Tiny took three awkward model-like steps, then strutted back to where we stood. "As you can see, I'm surviving just fine."

Danielle clapped like Tiny had just won an award.

Tiny and Danielle did some lame handshake that ended with a "whoop-whoop."

Julius was quiet for a second, then busted out laughing.

Tiny made a face at him, then eyed the statue. "What is that thing anyway?"

"It's for Tia's grandma," Julius said.

"Hmm, I know exactly where ugly stuff like that comes from," Danielle said. "Tia, is your grandma hanging with those voodoo-hoodoo people again?"

Tiny laugh-snorted, which annoyed me almost as much as Danielle's comment. "I call them the doo-doo's!" she said. "Are you one too?"

My face flushed immediately, and I was sure my entire head glowed like some weird orb.

"What? No!" I said, then turned toward Danielle. "And it's not voodoo. But even if it was, so what?"

"Whatever. Just tell us," Danielle cooed. "Your grandma a voodoo priestess?" She eyed Julius but continued to speak to me. "Could she put a love spell on someone?"

"No!"

"No to which one?" Tiny said. She removed a big pack of

sunflower seeds from a designer handbag. If I resembled a bird the way she did, I'd never eat any kind of seed.

"To both," I croaked.

Tiny cracked a shell in her mouth. "Well," she said, "can she give me the winning lottery numbers then? Or, since you're a priestess junior, can you give them to me?"

I opened my mouth, but my brain exploded with embarrassment and prevented me from thinking of any kind of comeback.

"Hello, why're you just staring at me?" Tiny torpedoed the empty shells from her mouth. "Can. You. Hear. Me. PJ? Get it? PJ? It's short for your new name, Priestess Junior."

Both Danielle and Tiny roared with laughter.

My face burned with humiliation, and I pretended not to pay attention. I wondered why Gram couldn't shop at regular stores like most everyone else in our neighborhood.

Danielle moved closer to Julius and placed her arms over his shoulders like she wanted to slow dance. Her wrists hung loose, and her gold bangle bracelets slid down and made a small clinking sound. "Are you busy later? Want to hang out?"

I turned away at the sight of them so close and pumped my inhaler even though I didn't need it that bad.

From the corner of my eye, I caught Julius just as he stepped aside. Danielle's arms flopped against her thighs.

"Later?" Julius said. "Um, can't. I'm busy."

When my face warmed up again, it was because I realized I had been the reason why he couldn't.

He looked to me, and I knew he wanted to be rescued,

but it was exactly what he had asked for with all that "good smelling" talk, so I watched as he squirmed and hoped he had learned his lesson.

"My mom always has stuff for me to do," Julius continued. "She's got a list and everything."

"Serious?" Danielle said, disappointed.

Tiny had stuffed a handful of seeds into her mouth. When she was done with each one, she spit it out. The empty shells littered the sidewalk. One that looked like a mole stuck to her chin.

"Not me, no way," Tiny said, after she popped open another shell. "My mom makes a list, then she's taking care of that list. I'm no kind of servant."

Danielle reached out and squeezed Julius's shoulder like a melon. "Okay, maybe we can get together another time."

"Yeah . . . okay," he said, then changed the subject. "So, who's stupid?"

"Amelia. She sent Joey some tacky photos showing off way too much skin, and he sent them to his friends and who knows who else."

"Wait," Julius said. "Joey as in big-mouth-can't-keep-a-secret-for-his-life Joey?"

"If you ask me, Joey's the stupid one for sharing them," I said. Julius nodded in agreement.

Tiny rolled her eyes then looked thoughtful, like she'd come up with something clever to add, but instead she cackled, and soon it turned into a wild coughing fit. A seed had gotten sucked down her throat.

Danielle pounded Tiny's narrow back and propelled a slick, wet seed, shell and all, from Tiny's mouth. It headed straight for Julius's cheek like a guided missile, and instead of sliding off, the seed sat there like a big, slick cockroach.

# Chapter Ten

Julius jumped around like his cheek had spontaneously combusted.

Having nearly choked to death didn't stop Tiny from howling with laughter while Danielle tried to catch Julius, who attempted to shake the seed free without touching it. He failed miserably and came close to knocking over the statue instead.

"Watch out!" I yelled.

I rescued it just in time.

Danielle grabbed hold of Julius with both hands. "Stay still," she said. "I'll get it!"

I wasn't crazy about how Danielle touched Julius, but I also was not about to take the seed off either. You have to choose your battles in life.

Danielle used her long manicured fingernail, the one with a gold heart in the middle, to scrape the seed off.

"You're such a baby, Julius," Tiny managed.

Julius lifted his shirt and used it to wipe his cheek. He glared at Tiny. "Eww," he said. "You're disgusting. Why do you have to eat those things anyway? Makes you look like, I don't know, the world's biggest bird."

Insulting Tiny had been a bad idea even though Danielle

was, as Gram would say, "gaga," over Julius. I expected her to use him like a human mop. But instead, she absentmindedly twirled a section of long, straight hair between her fingers.

"Shut up, Julius!" Tiny said when no one else spoke up. Then she turned to Danielle in a huff. "Come on! I'm hungry. Let's go inside. I'll tell my mom to make us something."

Tiny opened her front door, then stopped when she realized Danielle hadn't followed. "I said come on! I'm hungry!"

Finally, Danielle snapped out of her weird trance. "Relax, I'm coming."

"See you later, Julius," said Danielle, walking backward until she disappeared into the house.

"See you never, PJ!" Tiny said before she slammed the door.

That made me so mad, I wished she was right. If I were a priestess, I would have cast a spell to keep her beak shut forever.

I blew it off as best as I could, then turned to Julius. "Jeez, could she be any more obvious?"

"What?"

"Danielle likes you. You like her back?" I said. I needed to hear the answer.

He closed the gap between us, then took away the statue. "You know I don't," he said. His arm brushed mine and sent a crazy flutter to every part of my body, from the tips of my ears, to my chest, then down to my toes.

The feeling gave me hope that everything would be okay, that the *limpia* would work.

———————

A block away from home, we ran into Miss Smith and her traveling cigarette cloud.

"Have you heard any news?" she asked. Miss Smith adjusted an old-fashioned pink hair curler beneath a colorful headscarf. "It's a shame something like that happened to such a fine-looking man."

I had no idea how she could talk about a dead man being handsome. I took one last breath of smoke-free air, then hurried a few feet past her.

The three of us began walking toward home, with me and Julius slightly ahead of Miss Smith.

"What's the rush?" Miss Smith said.

"No rush," Julius said. "It's just that this statue is heavy, and we have to get it to Tia's grandmother."

Miss Smith gaped at the statue as though Julius held onto a squirming Medusa.

"Hey Tia, before I forget," she said. "When that cute detective is done talking to your parents, you send him to me. I don't have anything to say about who killed that man, but I wouldn't mind looking into that detective's eyes for a little while. I've always had a thing for redheads."

"Err . . . TMI," Julius whispered.

I tripped over my own feet and stumbled to a stop. Miss Smith and Julius stopped along with me.

"The detective . . . he's in my house?"

Miss Smith fanned herself with a copy of the *New York Daily News*. The headline sprang out at me and set the beat of my heart on double time:

*Vault manager for armored car company murdered on Brooklyn street. $2.5 million missing en route to local casino. Police launch massive search.*

Beneath that was a photo taken outside the armored car company's building, along with what looked like employees in uniform and lots of police officers.

My stomach flip-flopped like a fish caught in a net.

"Uh-huh," Miss Smith answered.

"Why?" I squeaked.

"About the murder, of course. He's questioning everybody in the neighborhood, and rumor has it he might have a lead."

Before I could get any more information, Miss Smith sashayed down the block and left me to make my own paranoid conclusions. The detective knew I saw the whole thing and did nothing but cowardly watch a man die. He was probably waiting to drag me into the interrogation room at the police station while the whole neighborhood watched. Now the killer's plan to shut me up would become a lot less complicated. He'd probably head straight for my parents as a warning for me to keep my mouth shut, or maybe he'd go after Gram, since she'd be a weaker target. No candle or statue could help her then. One hard shove or punch would hurt Gram really bad and maybe even kill her.

I felt like I might puke all over Mr. Elliot's small, manicured lawn. I bent over but my dry heaves failed to bring anything up.

"What's wrong, Tia?" Julius said. "Are you okay?"

I straightened up. "Um . . . yeah," I lied.

We walked the rest of the way home in silence. My stomach was uneasy the whole way.

When we were close enough to our block, I made out a crowd of people near the spot where the man had collapsed and died. I didn't know what to think, but when we reached them, I knew right away what was happening. A memorial for the dead man had sprouted.

# Chapter Eleven

Nervously, I stood among the crowd. I couldn't scrutinize the entire crowd for the killer and, for all I knew, he could be tucked in among the mourners, watching for me.

I thought about holding Julius's hand, but he still carried the statue. So, I did the next best thing. I circled my arm around his waist and latched onto the belt loop of his jeans. He didn't look directly at me, but I could still see his smile.

"Wow, look at all this stuff," Julius said.

Bouquets of flowers lay on top of one another, three rows deep. People passed by us to add their own tributes. People of every color gathered in silence as one. A man with a thick black brace over his knee held on to a purple leash. A short distance away, a small, fluffy black dog wearing a purple harness sniffed at the bottom of a tree. Its short, stubby tail quickly rocked side to side like whatever it smelled was the best thing ever. When the man placed his hand over his heart, I saw that his pinky was crooked and pointed in an odd direction. A younger dark-skinned woman with short, curly hair and designer sunglasses patted the man's back. Two Jewish men wearing yarmulkes stood shoulder to shoulder with a waiter from Georgie's, the nearby 24-hour diner.

A little boy with skinny legs and missing front teeth made his way to the center of the memorial, then placed a raggedy stuffed dog next to a photo of a man.

"Don't worry, Mommy. Boxer will take good care of Jonathan in heaven," he said, when he made his way back. His mom kneeled, then gripped him in an almost crushing embrace. A high-pitched squeal escaped from the little boy's lips.

"Too hard, Mama!" he squeaked.

I tried to drive away the sadness all around me. I swallowed until my mouth was a desert, but it didn't work. For a split second, I wished I had gone to camp. Uncontrolled tears rained down and left dime-sized dots on the front of my blue shirt.

The man I had watched draw his last breath had a name. Jonathan.

I stepped away from Julius and approached the little boy and his mom. I didn't know what I would say, or why I had even gone over to them.

I waited for the mom to stand before I said hello.

"Did you know him?" I said. "Jonathan, I mean?"

"Yes, we did. He was—"

"The best snowman maker on Pioneer Street!" the little boy chimed in.

The mom placed her hand on the boy's cheek. "Yes, he was, sweetie." Then she turned to me. "He was our neighbor and used to take Charlie sledding every year at first snow. He . . . ," she swallowed hard and went silent. Then, "Did you know him, too, honey?" she finished.

Pioneer Street was only two blocks from my house. I'd

probably passed Jonathan a million times around the neighbor-hood. A lump formed in my throat and grew and kept me silent.

The mom stroked my cheek and wiped away my tears. She smiled weakly. "I know, I know," she said. "This is all so very hard."

I stumbled through the throng of people and searched for Julius. He wasn't where I'd left him.

From somewhere behind me came, "Hey, Tia, wait up!"

I used the neck of my T-shirt to dry my eyes before I turned around. Marco jogged over to me.

"You okay?" he said.

"I guess."

Marco shoved his hands deep inside his pants pockets. He was so slim, the pants drooped with the extra weight.

"I was wondering if you, I mean if we . . . ," he said.

It seemed like he had forgotten what he wanted to say and after an awkward minute, he blurted out, "Never mind."

I watched as he quickly walked toward some boys from school, then disappeared among them.

It wasn't too long before I found myself face to face with Jonathan—Jonathan Davis, to be exact. A photo of him rested on an easel that was almost as tall as I was. Jonathan wore an army uniform and a wide smile. Not only was he young and strong, but brave too. In that moment of his life, he probably thought he'd live forever. His big, blue movie-star eyes seemed to beg me to speak up. They pleaded with me to help him rest in peace by telling what I saw because he couldn't.

Just then the man with the dog walked up alongside me. His

short-cropped hair glistened with sweat. Except for sniffling, he had been quiet. My heart dove. I thought that maybe he was part of Jonathan's family.

I searched for something pleasant to say, but I knew no such words existed.

The dog turned her attention to my feet, her tail less excited, but it still got a workout.

When the man began going through his pants pockets, a battered plastic identification card fell to the ground faceup. Seeing his thick knee brace, I quickly bent down to pick it up for him.

"Here you go"—I read the name off the card—"Mr. Butler."

He wiped at his eyes with a napkin from the House of Pizza. "Thanks," he said.

The dog yelped and wagged her stubby tail.

"It's okay, Potato," Mr. Butler said.

"That's a great name," I said.

Mr. Butler gave his tired eyes one last swipe. "Thank you. I mostly call her Sweet Potato, for obvious reasons."

"Can I pet her?" I said.

I would've given anything to have a dog, but my parents thought it wasn't a good idea because of my asthma. Even though I had done a ton of research and found lots of breeds that didn't shed and had low dander, they wouldn't take the chance.

As if on cue, Potato let out another yelp.

"Absolutely," Mr. Butler said. "She loves love."

Then it was my turn for licks. Her soft tongue was hot and

very wet. It wasn't long before my hand had been slathered in slimy dog spit.

"Was he . . . I mean is he . . . ," I restarted after a few seconds, like I had mush for brains. I tried again, "Was Jonathan a family member?"

I held my breath and waited for an answer.

"Oh no, I don't have any family of my own, but Jonathan treated me like a brother." Mr. Butler sighed deeply, then continued. "Jonathan was one in a million. He didn't deserve this, and no one will do a thing about it. No one."

A guilty pang shot through my chest like my heart had released it full force. I turned away for a few seconds and waited for Mr. Butler's words to fade into the humid air, but they clung to me. I was no one.

I wiped my wet hand on my shorts. Mr. Butler's weary eyes drooped with sorrow.

"And if no one speaks up, the killer will get away with it." Mr. Butler put his free hand on my shoulder and squeezed.

A minute went by before he continued. "What's your name?"

I told him, and he asked if I lived nearby.

I nodded. I wanted to keep the exact location a secret. It would be painful for him to know I had been so close to where Jonathan had died. He might ask if I had seen anything out of the ordinary that night, and with the way Mr. Butler smiled so tenderly at me, I couldn't trust myself to keep any kind of information from him.

Mr. Butler tucked the crumpled napkin into his pants

pocket, then took my hand. His own hand was speckled with light-brown freckles. Despite the heat, it was cool to the touch. "Nice to meet you, Tia."

Potato patiently watched the activity. So many people came and went. Some read every tribute, others just curiously passed through.

Mr. Butler continued. "I live close to where Jonathan lived, on Pioneer Street. Used to think that was a funny name for a street. It made me think of early settlers and now I'm settled right in the middle of it."

"How'd you meet Jonathan?" I said.

"Oh, we both volunteered at the animal shelter on Van Brunt Street," he said. "That's where Miss Sweet Potato here came from. It was love at first sight."

Potato looked up excitedly at the sound of her name and I could see how loving her had been easy.

"Jonathan made sure to come by and walk Potato for me ever since I twisted my knee two months ago." Mr. Butler gestured toward his knee brace. It was the kind I'd seen for sale at the pharmacy, right next to the ACE bandages. "He was a friend right up until the very end."

It was hard to listen to how great Jonathan was, and part of me wanted to walk away, but that would've been rude, so I stuck it out.

"The day he . . . this all happened, we were supposed to meet at the pizza shop."

I choked back tears. "What happened?"

"I waited around for fifteen minutes and when he didn't show, I left, went home, and made a peanut butter sandwich."

Mr. Butler was quiet as he fiddled with Potato's leash. I worried I'd upset him even more by the questions I had asked and was about to say goodbye when he straightened his collar and continued.

"Jonathan was a sharp dresser too," he said. "No matter what, he just shined brighter than everyone else."

I halfheartedly grinned along with Mr. Butler.

"He even kept an extra shirt and tie at work just in case. I told him it'd be easier to wear a baby bib."

When I laughed that time, it was genuine.

"Where'd he work?" I said.

"Oh, um . . . don't exactly know. Asked him once, but he sidestepped the question every which way till Sunday and Monday. If there's one thing I can do, it's take a hint, so I dropped it."

I wanted to know more about Jonathan, like if he had family, or if Mr. Butler ever met any of his other friends. But before I got the chance to ask, we were interrupted by the woman I had seen Mr. Butler with earlier. Her sunglasses sat on top of her head and reflected the bright-blue sky.

"Aaron? I've been looking for you," she said. "Are you okay?"

"As okay as I'll ever be, Elaine."

"Well, I'm on my way back. Do you want me to wait for you?"

Mr. Butler adjusted his brace and grimaced. "Yes, I could

use the company." Then he turned to me and said, "It was nice talking to you, Tia."

"Mr. Butler?" I said as they began moving away.

"Yes?"

"I can come over later and walk Potato for you. I mean if you want me to."

Walking Potato was small and simple and definitely didn't take away any of the guilt, but it was something I could actually do to help.

Both he and Elaine smiled. "That'd be wonderful," Mr. Butler said. "She'd like that."

He gave me his address, then they were on their way.

I never knew either of my grandpas, but as I stood and watched Mr. Butler slowly limp through the horde of people, I couldn't help but hope that they would've been exactly like him.

# Chapter Twelve

"Tia?" Julius said, suddenly beside me.

"There you are," I said.

I weaved a path out of the crowd.

Julius followed. "Who was that guy?"

"Mr. Butler," I said, then nodded toward where the memorial stood. "Jonathan used to walk his dog for him. They were friends, but now . . . anyway, I told him I could walk her later."

"Wow, really?" Julius said. "That was nice of you."

When we got to my house, I ignored the now-smeared yellow words on the sidewalk and slowly pushed open the front door. Even though it was only one thirty in the afternoon, dinner already simmered on the stove. The smell of Gram's famous chili filled the air with spicy goodness. Normally, I would've been excited, because Gram could seriously cook, but that day, I thought about the pizza Mr. Butler and Jonathan were supposed to share, and the smell only made me nauseous. I wondered if he'd think about Jonathan at every meal for the rest of his life. The thought of that made me want to visit Mr. Butler the first chance I got. I was determined to do what I could for him. I didn't kill Jonathan, but I hadn't done anything to help catch his killer either, the person who had cost Mr. Butler his best friend.

The flame from the candle on the table flickered steadily. The toes of Gram's sandals were neatly tucked beneath the table.

Voices floated in from inside the kitchen. I tried to make out what they were saying but couldn't hear anything.

"This thing is stretching my arms. Go inside," Julius said from behind me.

I pushed the door open fully. "Okay, okay," I said.

I placed my house keys next to the candle just as Gram shuffled in wearing her hot-pink *chanclas*. Gram loved her slippers and kept a backup pair at our house.

"Did you get it, *mi amor?*"

"Yes," I said.

Gram wore the flowered apron I had made for her at the mall when I was ten. For weeks, I had saved up every penny I earned doing chores around the house. I even took up garbage duty, which relieved my much-appreciative dad. The guy at the mall stand where I had the apron made cracked up when I handed him a photo of me puckering up like a duck with chapped lips, thanks to a mouth ringed in Mom's new Boundless Red lipstick. The caption beneath the photo read: Kiss the Cook.

The photo had faded some but was still visible. Even though the apron held on by a thread, Gram insisted that no matter what, she'd keep it forever.

"Gram," Julius said, "where should I put this?"

Gram smiled lovingly, then slid the candle over to make room for the statue. "Put him right here."

Julius did what he was told, then swung out his arms. "Those botanica people sure are strange, Gram."

Gram arranged Archangel Michael. "Hmm?" she said.

I was afraid Julius would say something about me going behind the curtain, which would lead to a million questions, so I nudged him and gave a quick headshake. He understood and didn't say anything more.

Just then Mom called, "Tia come to the kitchen, please. There's a detective here who wants to ask you a few questions."

Gram shuffled back into the kitchen as happy as could be. Our protector had been placed on guard duty. I, on the other hand, began to sweat, knowing that I was going to lie my way through whatever the detective asked, no matter what it was.

"Tia?" Mom called out again and sounded a little more impatient. "Did you hear me?"

"Be right there," I said, then began a deep-breathing exercise I had learned in health class. It was supposed to be ten slow breaths in and out, but I didn't have that kind of time. Plus, Julius interrupted me after just two.

"Come on Tia, what're you waiting for? I want to tell him about Big Mike."

I grasped his arm as he tried to move past me. "No," I whispered. "It wasn't Big Mike."

"What? How do you know?"

"Tia!" Mom's voice rang out and caused me to jump.

"I just do, Julius. Please, trust me." I started toward the kitchen. "Coming, Mom."

Julius followed quietly, but I felt his questioning eyes as they burrowed into my back.

In the kitchen, the detective's suit jacket hung from his

chair almost to the floor. A small, stubby gun rested securely in the holster on his side. I had always thought cops carried big guns. I didn't know why that was. I wondered if he had ever shot anyone, and if small guns made as much noise as big ones did. With knives, I knew size didn't matter. As long as the blade pierced something important, a life could be cut down, causing family and friends to wake up to the most horrible news anyone could imagine. I shuddered and fought the urge to run into Mom's arms.

Julius leaned against the sink and studied me like he expected an explanation, but I managed to ignore his questioning gaze.

Mom's special coconut flan sat on the kitchen table. It was Dad's favorite dessert, and we almost always had it in the house. Mom said she'd made it so many times she could prepare it with her eyes closed. The flan was made with evaporated milk, coconut cream, something called condensed milk, eggs, vanilla extract, and sugar. It's a Latino version of custard, only better.

Mom tapped the vacant chair next to her. "Have a seat."

My legs wobbled from nerves and it felt good to sit, but sitting didn't stop them from knocking against each other.

"This is Detective Erickson," Mom said.

It was the same man who had questioned everyone outside that morning. The one with the shiny brown shoes.

"He's investigating the murder of that poor man."

I wanted to tell Mom that he wasn't just a poor man. That he had a name. He was Jonathan.

The detective had a huge hunk of half-eaten flan in front

of him. He wiped beads of moisture from his splotchy pink face with Mom's special napkins she only used on holidays and for important company. The soft, light-blue material turned dark with sweat, and I half expected to see some of the pink from his face smeared onto it too. I wondered what Mom thought about Detective Erickson using it as a sweat rag.

"This is my daughter, Tia, and her friend, Julius, who lives next door."

Detective Erickson reached out and shook my hand, and even though it wasn't the hand he used to wipe his head with, it was damp and a little bit sticky. As soon as I got the chance, I sneaked my hand beneath the table and dried it off on my shorts.

Julius stepped away from the sink for his turn to shake Erickson's hand. When Julius thought no one was looking, he gave his palm a quick rub against the leg of his jeans, then resumed his spot at the sink.

The detective placed the damp napkin across his thigh. "Nice to meet you both," he said. "Now, do either of you know anything about the murder that occurred?"

"Why're you asking us?" I said before I thought it through.

"Well," the detective said, "I'm asking everyone, not just you." If he had been shocked at my tone, he didn't show it. They probably taught stuff like that in detective training or something. "Never let them know what you're thinking" was good advice. I intended to do the same.

I tried to read Erickson's face for clues, but it was emotionless. Another useful piece of advice, I thought. I only hoped I could pull it off as well. For all I knew, I had already incriminated myself somehow.

Sweat began to roll long and slow behind my ears but I couldn't do anything about it without looking guilty of something. Sweating that way made me think about a snowstorm that hit a couple of years before. Brooklyn had gotten ten inches of snow. As soon as the storm let up, Julius and I threw on our winter gear, then dove into the nearest snowdrift. Our hands were so close, they almost touched. And even though it was freezing outside, I wasn't cold at all. Beneath my wool cap, my head began to sweat, starting the very same way.

"No idea, detective," Julius said.

I forced myself to make eye contact with Erickson. "Me neither, but don't you have a lead already?"

"I'd rather not discuss that," he said.

The detective began to scratch words onto a yellow notepad alongside words already there. I tried to make them out, but the letters were miniature and impossible to read.

Finally, Erickson lifted his head from the pad. "It might be something small, something you might not even think of as important. Is there anything at all that you can remember?"

The longer Erickson stayed, the more I worried the killer might get wind that he questioned me. I quickly shook my head.

I needed Erickson out of my house, and fast.

# Chapter Thirteen

Erickson adjusted himself in the chair. "Is there anything you can remember from that night?" he repeated.

I pretended to think hard about Erickson's question.

"Hmm . . . ," I said, finally. "No, nothing."

"Your asthma was bothering you last night, right, Tia?" Erickson asked. "My son had it when he was four years old but, thankfully, grew out of it. I know just how scary it can be."

I glanced at Mom and tried to figure out what else she told him about me. "Yes," I said.

"Did it keep you awake at all?"

I ran my hand over the pocket of my shorts and felt the small bottle Celia had given me. I promised myself that as soon as the detective left, I'd take a bath using some of the liquid. "A little," I said.

Erickson's annoying interrogation continued, and I felt like we were playing a game of ping-pong. "What time were you awake?"

Even before I answered, he began to scribble in his pad again.

"How should I know? I'm not a human clock." I only meant

to think it, not actually say it, and the minute it came out of my mouth, I knew I'd be in big trouble with Mom.

Julius spit out a laugh, but he was the only one in the room amused.

Erickson lifted his head. The splotches had reappeared. His eyes went flat and showed no sign of what he thought. Those training classes had been worth their weight in gold.

"Tia!" Mom shouted. "You apologize to Detective Erickson right now."

Gram was silent but watched me closely. She made me more uncomfortable than Erickson did. I wanted to tell her that I'd lose it if he kept questioning me.

"Sorry," I whispered. "I have no idea what time it was."

"Apology accepted," Erickson smirked.

Mom never took her eyes off me. "I'm also sorry, detective."

I knew I had not only embarrassed her but disappointed her, too, and I felt horrible about it.

"No worries, Mrs. Lugo," Erickson said, then turned his attention back to me.

"So, you don't have a clock in your room?"

Mom's face twitched and spoke silently to me. Her lips thinned out and her eyes grew large with warning. *Watch your tone.*

"Yeah, I do, but I didn't pay any attention to the time."

"Did you hear anything?" Erickson continued.

"No."

"Did you look out of your window at all?"

I shook my head and watched as Erickson wrote in his pad.

"Did you take your medicine?"

I had no idea what my medicine had to do with a murder. "Yeah," I said, careful not to drag out the *ah* sound with attitude.

"Was it an inhaler?" Erickson said. "My son hated to use his."

"Yes," I said.

"Did you take a drink of water afterward? My son said it helped with the taste."

I felt like I was the criminal. "Uh, I think I did."

"You said you didn't look out of the window, right?" Erickson said.

My stomach felt nervous and I thought had to use the bathroom. *Enough, enough, enough* went around and around inside my head.

"Right," I said. I did my best to keep my voice even.

I thought about the statue by the front door and hoped it could protect me from Erickson.

"Because," the detective said as he rocked his pen between his index and middle fingers, "there's a bottle of water on your windowsill, and I'm wondering if you're absolutely positive that you didn't—"

A bomb had been dropped. The only way he would've known that was if he had been inside my bedroom. The thought of him as he snooped around my private things freaked me out.

"I already told you," I said, "I didn't look out the window!"

"That's it, Tia," Mom said. "You've just lost your cell for a week and if you keep being disrespectful, I'll make it the entire month."

My face flushed with embarrassment.

"Detective," Mom said, "please excuse Tia for a moment while she retrieves her phone."

There was no arguing; I deserved it. I did as I was told and delivered the phone into Mom's waiting palm.

If Mom noticed the Band-Aid covering the lens of the camera, she didn't mention it.

Erickson clicked and unclicked his pen. Finally, he thanked us for our time, then stood to leave.

"Anytime, Detective," Mom said.

"Would you like to stay for dinner, Detective?" Gram said.

"I wish I could, but thanks for the invite."

Relief spread through me. I knew I'd never make it through a whole meal with him dissecting my every word.

"Maybe another time, then," Gram said.

Erickson handed me a plain business card. "Here's my card. Call me if you remember anything. Night or day, it doesn't matter. We need the killer off the streets and the sooner, the better."

Mom and Gram walked Erickson to the door. I tossed the card onto the kitchen counter as soon as they were out of sight. I wanted to throw it into the trash can because there was no way I'd ever call him, but I knew Mom would've only fished it out.

"Welp," Julius said, "that was intense."

He had no idea.

I opened the refrigerator door and pretended to look for something. I knew Julius would ask me about Big Mike again, and I hoped to stall long enough for Mom and Gram to come back.

"So?"

I played dumb from inside the fridge. "So, what?"

"Come on, T, you know what I mean. Why do you think Big Mike is innocent?"

"Because I think he's all talk and no action, that's all."

"When did you start believing that?"

"A couple of incidents doesn't make you—"

"A murderer?" Julius said.

I moved around the jar of pickles and searched for the impossible: a way to make Julius let it go. "Please, just stop."

"I can't," Julius said. "Something's up. Tell me what you know"—Mom and Gram entered the kitchen just in time to witness Julius's impersonation of Detective Erickson—"about the murder," he finished.

"Who knows what about the murder?" Gram said.

I'm not proud of what I did next, but I absolutely had to change the subject. There was just no other way.

# Chapter Fourteen

While still standing by the open refrigerator, I shoved an industrial sized jar of cherries off the shelf. I knew there'd be nothing like a massive, messy explosion and spill to get a conversation to go another direction. I knew it would be bad, but I hadn't expected just how awful it turned out to be. Or how remorseful and scared I'd feel afterward.

"Tia! Are you okay?" Mom shrieked and rushed to my side, her slippers soaking up cherry juice.

"I think so," I said.

Cherry juice mixed with shards of glass splattered across the entire kitchen floor. Even part of the living room was bathed in a sharp, red mess.

"*Ay dios mío!*" Gram said.

"What?" My voice was a high-pitched squeal.

"Tia, just d–don't move," Julius said. He held out his hands, palms toward me. "And do not look down."

I had no idea why everyone was freaking out, but when I saw the way Mom's eyes grew way too large for a cherry mess, I panicked. "What's wrong?" I said.

"Just don't move."

"You're scaring me." My voice quivered even though I fought to keep calm.

I gazed past my leg, down to my foot, where a sliver of glass stood at attention in the space between my third and fourth toes. Blood began soaking into the fake fur of my flip-flop. That's when the pain of fifty beestings rushed to my brain as if I had unleashed the bees by just looking. "MOM?"

"It's okay, baby," Mom said, in a composed voice. "I'll get it out. Just stay still, okay?"

When Mom gripped the tip of the glass poking from my skin, I turned away. There was a pinch, and then it was out.

Gram headed to the bathroom for emergency supplies.

Julius turned toward the sink and gagged into it. "Should I call 911?" he asked when he was done.

"No ambulance. I'm okay. Right, Mom?" I said. I felt like I had suddenly morphed into a whiny five-year-old.

Mom took my hand. "Yes," she said. "You're going to be fine. There's no need for an ambulance."

When Gram returned, she handed Mom a sterile patch of gauze, the brown bottle of the peroxide I hated so much, a bandage, and a small jar filled with something that looked like Vaseline, only it was bright green instead of clear. No writing and no label on the jar meant it was special botanica stuff. Our house had was filled with these label-less items.

Back when Julius and I first started to hang out, he needed an aspirin, so I sent him to the bathroom medicine cabinet. I was so embarrassed when he came out with the weirdest look on his face.

"What?" I said.

"Um, nothing."

"Did you find the aspirin?"

Julius rubbed his temples. "I don't need the aspirin anymore. My headache is almost gone."

I knew he was lying by the way he avoided looking at me. "There's a lot of weird stuff in there and . . . ," he said.

I had forgotten about Gram's botanica concoctions placed neatly on a shelf inside the medicine cabinet. Just a year before, Mrs. Moore had begun renting an apartment next door. She always argued with everyone on our block—except for us. Gram said it was because of the black salt she sprinkled outside our house. It was used to protect against bad neighbors. A large bottle of it took up space right next to a special body wash, which was supposed to deflect bad wishes people had for you. The bottle of salt featured an illustration of a tornado, like the kind drawn in comics, and bold red letters that said *Destroy Everything*. Gram explained that *everything* only meant problematic situations and negative people. Mrs. Moore moved away after only four months. Gram hadn't been sure which of the mixtures worked, so she vowed to always use them together. She called it a double dose of "see you later."

By the look on Julius's face, I was sure the jar filled with the pulverized-eggshell mixture was what had done him in, especially because the smell of it sometimes slipped out from underneath the jar's cap.

Of course, Gram had a use for those eggshells too. One day after dinner, I'd overheard Dad telling Mom and Gram that the company he worked for had begun downsizing. He worried he'd be let go. Mom told him we'd get through whatever was coming but Gram remained silent.

For two weeks, Gram had us save all our eggshells. She even had Mom do extra baking so that we'd use more eggs. For those weeks, our lunches consisted of egg-salad sandwiches. Dad had just about had enough of it when Gram declared we had what was needed. Then she got to work as I watched.

Gram added peanuts, sugar, and ashes to the eggshells. As she combined everything in a big metal bowl, she pointed out how it went beyond stirring and mashing the things she had collected. She had also added things you couldn't see or touch. Love and good intention. For those two, she placed her hands near her heart, then gently placed the invisible items inside the bowl with the rest of the ingredients. This ritual was for Dad, but he didn't know it. One month later, not only did Dad stay with the company, but he got a promotion too.

But that first time I'd had Julius over, I'd almost died of humiliation. It was like I could see my family through Julius's eyes, and I didn't like what I saw. I couldn't hide anything from him and there was no lie I could tell. I had no choice but to share the embarrassing background of each of the jars.

Julius left soon after, and I wondered if he'd tell everyone at school how weird my family was for having our medicine cabinet loaded with botanica stuff. But after a week, I didn't hear a word or a snicker about it. That week turned into two, and when we approached three, I knew I was safe.

Now, Gram's shaggy gray eyebrows bunched together and

almost formed a unibrow. She pointed to the jar. "This will help with the pain," she said.

Mom slowly slipped off my flip-flop.

While Mom examined my foot, Gram grasped my hand and rubbed the top of it with her thumb. "*Estás bien*," she whispered.

I wasn't sure anything would ever be okay again, but when Gram and I locked eyes, I knew she was right. I was okay, at least for that moment.

My mind wandered and I thought about Gram's life and the things she'd done in her seventy-five years. The stories I'd heard about how she'd take any job she could get, and how in tenth grade, her last day of school ever, her best friends, Magdalena and Louise, cried. Gram's dad had died, leaving her mom struggling to pay the bills. Gram volunteered, against her mother's wishes, to quit school and work full time, and she never went back.

I choked up when I thought about how lucky I was to have the Gram I had. The idea of her being taken away from me almost caused a breakdown. I kissed her soft cheek and she responded with kisses of her own. I nuzzled into her neck and stayed there a few seconds longer. Her sweet scent comforted me like it always had.

"All done, Tia," Mom said. "You're going to be just fine."

Julius tiptoed over for a peek but didn't fully commit to a closer look. "Really?" he said, as if he'd expected half my foot to be a dangling mess.

"Yes," Mom said as she examined the cut, then swiped it

with peroxide again. "It's not as bad as it looked. Now, how exactly did that jar fall? Were your hands wet?"

"No," I said.

Mom kissed the top of my head and I hoped that meant she felt generous. "Does this mean I can have my phone back?"

"No way," Mom said.

"Can't blame a girl for trying."

Mom chuckled, then globbed some extra green goo over the top of my sore foot. After a minute, the house phone rang. I was pretty sure Julius and I were the only ones on our block who still had one. Ours was mustard yellow and hung on the wall next to the fridge. It was older than I was and looked it too.

Gram caught it before the third ring. "*Hola*," she said, then listened for a few seconds. "*Por qué?*"

She was only on for a little while longer before she hung up.

"Alex is going to be late tonight," Gram said. "Someone stole the bank deposit and he has to wait for the police to arrive."

"Well, this day just keeps getting stranger," Mom said.

Julius inched closer and gaped at my green-and-red glistening foot. "Eww, looks pretty disgusting," he said.

I couldn't argue. It looked like a sick-zombie Christmas ornament. "Mom, can you take some of that gunk off?"

"No," Gram said, "and the longer it stays on, the better."

Mom inspected the cut once more. "It's looking better already."

Mom placed the daggerlike glass not too far from where I sat on the counter. It was pointy and had just enough blood on the tip that my mind went right back to the night before. I had no idea whether or not Jonathan's parents were still around but that didn't stop me from thinking about how much they must've loved him. The same way Mom and Dad loved me. It wasn't long before my tears transformed into flowing twin rivers.

Gram kissed the top of my head. "*Mi amor*, please don't cry."

"All that blood made it look worse than it really is," Mom said. "Blood tends to do that."

How I wished that were true.

# Chapter Fifteen

Just as Mom wrung out the last of the cherry-drenched mop, Dad walked through the door. The smell of smoke wafted in behind him, which meant he'd blown out Gram's candle. He didn't say a word about our new protective statue.

Julius and I sat side by side on the couch. When Dad made his way toward the living room, Julius jumped to his feet like we had been doing something wrong. Our "Home Is Everything" pillow that rested on his lap fell to the floor. It was the very first needlepoint project Gram had ever completed.

"What's wrong?" I said.

Julius picked up the pillow. "Nothing, I just don't want your dad to think . . ."

"To think what?"

"You know, like, we're together or something."

Dad thought I was too young to date, but Mom and Gram disagreed. In their book, it was okay as long as things didn't get "too serious"—and they both made sure I knew what "too serious" meant. Unfortunately, they told me all this on the exact same morning I got my period for the very first time. Like I didn't have enough to worry about, I got "the talk." In Gram's words, my body had "joyously made the journey from childhood to womanhood and could make babies." *Make.* I pictured the hundreds of times I had made people out of Play-Doh or drawn armies of stick figures with mounds of hair and no flesh. I wanted to continue thinking about those things instead.

Just to make things a billion times worse, that day I got my period was also the first day of sixth grade. The night before my first day in a new school, I had laid out new clothes and couldn't wait to wear a pair of jeans I'd begged Mom for during summer break. They hugged whatever curves had shown up during the summer and I was thrilled. When I came out of the dressing room, Mom had cringed.

"No good," was her automatic response.

Gram's eyes welled up when she saw me, and I knew her happy tears would be my key to a big fat yes, and I had been right. But the tight denim was too uncomfortable because my stomach was ridiculously crampy and bloated, so I changed into loose-fitting sweatpants. I felt a lot better, but it wasn't exactly the impression I wanted to give on the first day of middle school. And just like I thought, the friendship slots filled up fast, and I had failed to make friends.

The only good thing about starting sixth grade was Julius.

Julius had moved into the house next to us the year before, but it wasn't like we hung out or anything, and as far as I could tell, he didn't have any friends either. Two days into a new school year though, we were in the same friendless boat—literally, which I didn't mind at all since he was so cute. I had only spied on him from my back porch up until then.

We were cruising the Hudson River on a "Getting to Know

You" boat trip the PTA put together for incoming sixth graders. I spotted Julius, who wore a light-blue polo shirt and a pair of neatly creased khakis, trying to make conversation with a group of boys, who had been drawn together like magnets as soon as we set foot on the boat. I watched as Julius failed to break through their magnetic field, and it was painful, but when they started to make fun of his stutter, I wanted to hurl them all overboard.

"W–what, what's up?" Julius said.

The head of the group, a kid shorter than Julius, mimicked him, cracking up his two friends.

A boy with bony ankles that peeked out from what looked like his little brother's pants clapped Julius on the back. "W–why d–don't y–you t–tell u–us?"

More laughter. Then, "By the time he tells us," the leader said, "we'll all be asleep!"

Julius took a step back and I hoped he was winding up the mother of all punches designed to land squarely on the leader's smirking mouth. But he didn't. He didn't even curse him out, which at least would've been something.

"N–nothing," Julius said.

Three more boys joined in, and a circle grew around Julius. The boat rocked and they pretended it had knocked them into him. That's when I knew I had to act fast. I stormed over to where they stood and poured the large cup of tropical fruit punch I had been drinking from on the leader's sparkling new sneakers.

"Hey, watch what you're doing!" he shrieked.

I took a step closer. "Why don't you try and make me?"

Another boy I had seen around my neighborhood joined in and pointed toward me. "You'd better be careful," he said, laughing. "She might put a spell on you!"

"What're you talking about?" the leader said, annoyed.

"Her grandma shops at the botanica, and she probably does too. You know they're all witches in there, right?"

And poof, my bravery had evaporated.

The leader studied me. "Really?" he said. "Well, that explains why she's so ugly!"

He probably would've gotten away with it if the music hadn't stopped suddenly, allowing for the welcoming speech to start. One of the chaperones immediately snaked his way through the crowd and pulled the leader away. Without him, all the other boys walked off. That left me and Julius, and I was too embarrassed to even look at him.

I was about to slink away when he said, "Thanks for doing that, and by the way, you're not ugly. Not by a long shot."

And just like that, our friendship was sealed.

Now Julius lobbed Gram's pillow at me. "Never mind."

"Hey, honey," Dad said. "What happened to your foot?"

"A cherry jar fell out of the fridge and cut me." My voice was thick with guilt. "But I'm fine. Mom and Gram fixed me up."

"Yeah, mainly just a big mess." Julius stretched his arms toward the ceiling. "I'm going home, Tia. I'll see you tomorrow, okay?"

"Don't leave. Come with me to walk Potato."

"Who?" Julius said.

"Mr. Butler's dog," I said.

"Oh, right. Can't, I promised Dad I'd help him with some stuff around the house."

"Now that I know who Potato is," Dad said, "who in the world is Mr. Butler?"

I told Dad all about how I met Mr. Butler and how nice both he and his dog were. I left out the part about how I could've helped save his friend and walking his dog meant nothing compared to what I'd done.

"Did you clear everything with Mom?"

"Not yet, but I will," I said.

After Julius left, Gram strode into the living room. She carried her wet slippers in a plastic grocery bag. "You're finally home," she said.

Dad placed a kiss on Gram's cheek. "*Bendición,* Mami. How was your day?"

In my family, when you greeted older people that way it was like placing a blessing on them. Most of all, it was an act of love.

"Just fine, thanks to our protector at the front door."

Dad hesitated. "About that," he said. "You know I don't believe in botanica stuff and I especially don't want a candle burning 24-7 in my house. Please bring it all home with you when you leave."

Gram didn't take Dad seriously at all. She smiled, then patted his shoulder as she passed. "You don't have to believe to be protected. I believe enough for all of us. Besides, Tia needs it. She doesn't look good lately."

My heart dipped inside my chest and I pretended not to see how Gram studied me.

I planned on doing my part by bathing in the liquid Celia gave me, but I couldn't help silently adding my hope to Gram's belief.

Dad shook his head wearily, which meant Gram had won by forfeit.

Gram walked toward the front door. *"Buenas noches*, I'll see you tomorrow."

The soft flicking of Gram's old-fashioned silver lighter made me smile. Gram relit the candle and it would burn until we all went to bed that night.

"Did you stop by the library today?" Dad said. "You should probably go soon, in case they fill whatever available spots they have open."

When I mentioned working at the library, it had been just something I said. I didn't have any real intention of actually doing it. Anyone could walk into the library, and that included the killer on my trail.

"I will," I said.

I followed Dad into the kitchen, where Mom had everything pulled out of the fridge. Sponge in hand, she scrubbed at a glass shelf.

"Mom, I can finish that if you want," I said, regretful.

"No, that's okay, honey. I'm almost done."

Dad kissed Mom. "Was it that bad?"

"It was, but I decided since everything had to be pulled out anyway, it made sense to just clean the entire fridge."

After Mom filled Dad in on the cherry eruption and they had settled down, I told Mom about Mr. Butler and how I had offered to walk Potato for him.

"Hmm, I don't know . . . ," Mom said.

"It's still early," Dad said. "I think it'll be okay."

"Plus," I quickly added, "Potato doesn't shed so there's no chance she'll bring on an asthma attack."

I studied Mom's face and tried to guess at what her answer might be, and for a few seconds I thought it would be a great big no, but she gave me permission.

"Yay, thanks! Can I go now?" I said.

"Yes, but I don't like the idea of you going inside Mr. Butler's apartment," Mom said. "It's not like we know him, so I want you to stay in the hallway and let him bring Potato to you."

"I second that," Dad said.

I reassured them that I'd abide by their rule.

Dad clicked on the television and turned to the six o'clock news. "Don't be too long, and be extra careful."

"I will," I said.

Walking to Mr. Butler's was much harder than I'd thought it'd be. I expected another warning around every turn, studied every face, and watched every car until it was out of sight. The walk was uneventful until Marco rounded the corner on his bike. He spotted me, then hopped off while the bike was still in motion.

He walked alongside me. "You catch how smooth that was?" he said.

I didn't think it was smooth at all. He stumbled a little and for a second, I thought he'd end up kissing the stained sidewalk.

"Yeah, so smooth," I said.

We walked in silence for a full block before Marco spoke again.

"So, have you been to the new movie theater yet?" he said.

I hadn't had time to think of normal stuff, not when the murder and keeping safe occupied my brain. I shook my head, but I didn't think Marco noticed, because he kept talking without missing a beat.

"I heard they put in those cool reclining seats," he said. "You can even order food."

Just up ahead, on Pioneer Street, a smaller memorial had been set up along a black wrought iron fence. I stopped walking. I needed to gather my courage before I witnessed another reminder of what I had done.

Marco hadn't realized I'd stopped and kept walking. "I was thinking maybe we . . ."

"I have to go," I said, distracted.

"Oh, okay," Marco said. "Maybe I'll catch up with you later."

As I grew closer to the memorial, it was easy to tell that the tall building inside the fenced-in area was where Jonathan had lived. Messages addressed to him had been written on everything from large pieces of cardboard to flimsy pieces of paper that blew in the breeze. I read through a few of the notes and learned from someone named Michele how the Fourth of July was never going to be the same again. Another was addressed to "Santa Claus Jon" and simply read *Thanks for filling in*. I knew the next message was from Mr. Butler even before I came to the signature, and my stomach grew queasy.

*You were the brother I never had. Until we meet again.*
*With much love and admiration,*
*Aaron Butler*

I wasn't sure how someone so loved could've turned up murdered.

# Chapter Sixteen

Mr. Butler's address was two doors down from Jonathan's apartment building. It wasn't long after I rang Mr. Butler's bell that he buzzed me inside.

The hallway lighting was dim and the air humid. The light fixture hummed and was obviously broken. Both things reminded me of the botanica and of Celia and the bath I'd take as soon as I got home.

As I made my way toward 1C, Mr. Butler's apartment, somewhere nearby a lighter flicked. Just as I passed 1B, I slipped on a wrinkle in the carpet and almost fell.

"Careful," a gruff voice said.

I froze mid-step, my body suddenly rigid with fear. Looking around frantically, I noticed a man standing near the top step of the staircase. Only his legs were visible, and his black pants and sneakers told me nothing of who he was, or what he might've looked like.

"Or you'll get hurt," he continued.

I ignored my shaky legs and slowly began to move closer to Mr. Butler's door. Instead of an ordinary apartment door, I saw safety.

The man sighed noisily, then said, "And nobody wants that."

I made it to Mr. Butler's door and knocked a little too hard, which caused Potato to go nuts. She may have been small, but she sounded fierce.

Thankfully, it didn't take long for Mr. Butler to open the door.

Mr. Butler held Potato in his arms. "Okay, sweet girl," he said. "Calm down, it's only Tia."

Potato promptly slathered Mr. Butler's face in wet dog kisses. Her pink tongue resembled a slice of baloney.

"That's right. I know we don't get much company," Mr. Butler said as he put Potato down. "But we do have to give Tia a chance to come inside."

At first, the idea to walk Potato had seemed perfectly safe, but as I stood outside the door of a stranger, I suddenly felt nervous. Mr. Butler appeared completely harmless and kind, yet I thought about what Julius said while we were in the botanica. Freaks stay undercover.

I looked over my shoulder and half expected the man from the staircase right behind me. Mom told me to not go inside Mr. Butler's, but she didn't know about the threatening stranger on the stairs.

Mr. Butler must've sensed my apprehension. "Are you all right?" he said.

I considered him for a few seconds and searched for signs of an evil fiend, but I saw only concern and kindness on his face. I looked beyond him and into his neat and tidy apartment, and

I saw nothing worrisome. It even smelled like fresh brownies, which made my stomach toss and turn like I was starved.

Torn, I teetered at the threshold until the man on the staircase coughed like he wanted to remind me he was there. I stepped through the doorway. I obeyed my parents' rule the best I could and left the door partly open just in case something went wrong.

Mr. Butler handed me a poop bag for cleanup, which was something I hadn't thought about, and Potato's leash. When I reached for it, Potato yelped and did a little circle dance, which made it nearly impossible for me to get it fastened.

"She's not like this with everyone," Mr. Butler said. "She must recognize something really special in you, Tia."

He couldn't have been more wrong. I had let a person die, and that made me a lot of things—none of them special.

I sat on the floor and hoped Potato would come to me, but it only seemed to encourage her to continue her funny two-legged dance. Mr. Butler and I had a great laugh over that, for which I was grateful. It helped me forget about the man on the staircase and everything else in my life.

"Are you showing off for Tia?" Mr. Butler said. "She might change her mind, you know."

"No way," I said. "She's adorable!"

Finally, Potato sat and waited as I secured her harness and leash.

When it was time to go, I worried that the man might still be at the top of the steps. Thankfully, Mr. Butler was concerned that Potato would give me a hard time, so he watched as we made our way out of the building.

Between visiting Mr. Butler and Potato's silly gallop, I was in the best mood I had been in since before the murder. It wasn't long before Potato and I dashed through Cat Park without a worry in the world. (It's actually called Catlyn Park, but with so many stray cats roaming around in it, we always call it Cat Park.)

For the entire walk, I managed to put the man on the staircase out of my mind, but when it came time to take Potato home, my hands began to sweat, and holding on to the leash made it worse.

When I reached Pioneer Street though, instant relief swept over me. I caught just the tail end of a man wearing the same black pants and shoes as he entered the passenger side of a red car. The driver sped away before I had a chance to see what the man looked like.

Back at Mr. Butler's, a plate of brownies and two tall glasses of milk waited for us. He motioned for me to have a seat across from him at the table.

From the doorway, I thought again about the rule I had broken. It was fine earlier and so I decided it'd be fine again. After all, Mr. Butler lost his best friend because of me, and I had to step up. It was the right thing to do.

The chair cushion was covered in thick, clear plastic and I knew my legs would be stuck to it when I stood. Mr. Butler offered me a huge brownie on a plate. "Made from scratch," he said.

I took a polite bite. The brownie was better than I'd hoped. It was extra crispy along the edges, and warm and mushy in the middle.

"This is the best brownie I've ever had," I said.

"It's my mother's recipe," Mr. Butler said after he'd swallowed a mouthful. "Maybe next time I'll make you a batch of her rice pudding."

Potato looked up at me from her bed as if she knew how glad I was that there'd be a next time. I smiled at her, sharing our own little secret.

Mr. Butler picked up his glass of milk, then held it toward me. "Cheers," he said.

I had never "cheered" anyone that way, but it didn't feel weird at all. I quickly swallowed the bite I had just taken, then held up my glass. "Cheers to your mom, and her delicious brownies."

We both took a swig of milk, then finished off two brownies each.

Potato licked my ankles as the three of us said our goodbyes, then I was on my way home.

The good feeling I had while at Mr. Butler's disappeared as soon as I reached the memorial outside of Jonathan's building. Two more people had secured tributes to the gate.

If it hadn't been for me, there'd be no memorial. No reason for tears and tributes, or for Mr. Butler's pain. I had been responsible for all of that, and no matter how many walks I'd take Potato on, it would never make up for the terrible thing I'd done.

I numbly made my way back home.

Mom and Dad had barely changed positions. I sat between them on the couch and told them all about Potato. I left out the part where I had broken their only rule. In this moment, I was safe, and at home. That was all that mattered.

Afterward, I thought about the man who had been outside the botanica and the man in Mr. Butler's hallway, and the urge to start the process with the stuff Celia gave me grew stronger. I could not put it off, because for all I knew, the killer already had a plan to take out my whole family. No amount of happiness could've changed that fact.

I excused myself and got ready for my bath.

While the bathtub filled up, I thought about the little boy and his mother whom I'd met at the memorial, but it was Mr. Butler who stayed with me. Whoever killed Jonathan had taken a piece of Mr. Butler, too, and I was partly to blame. I had to try and fill some of that void. It was the least I could do.

In the bathroom, I unscrewed the cap of the little bottle, took a big whiff, and regretted it right away. It smelled like wet dirt, which made me think of worms. Worms made me think of graves, and graves made me think of dead people. Jonathan.

I stared into the mirror and wished it all away until the simmering sobs finally bubbled up and over. My fluffy white towel absorbed every whimper.

When the tears had dried up, I got undressed, then threw my clothes into the hamper. I thought about taking off the beaded necklaces Celia gave me but figured it would only add to the power of the bath, so I left them on.

I held the bottle to the light and saw that there wasn't much liquid in it. I had to be careful and not use it up all at once.

I watched the syrupy yellow liquid blend in with the running water as I held the bottle over the tub. When the bath was full, it looked like an elephant had used it for a toilet. I certainly didn't want to bathe in it, that was for sure. But I had no other choice.

I dipped my foot into the water first, then waited for something to happen. There was no burning, itching, or anything else, so I eased completely into the tub and waited for the magic to begin. How it would happen, I had no clue. I thought a dramatic flash of lightning accompanied by some kind of supernatural swoosh would've been the perfect sign. But none of that happened.

The cool porcelain of the bathtub met my warm skin as I leaned back and tried to relax. After a few more minutes of nothing, I held my nose and dunked beneath the cloudy water. Maybe I had to be completely submerged for the magic to begin.

Instead, the killer's hush filled the eerie stillness, his finger pressed against his lips, and demanded I choose. Life or death? The memory of his blade glinted in the moonlight and reminded me that I wasn't safe, and maybe would never be again.

Gasping and coughing, I shot out of the tub like someone had been holding my head beneath the water. A wave sloshed over the side of the tub and created a puddle on the black-and-white tile floor.

I had taken safety for granted my whole life, and it had only taken seconds to be erased without a hint that it ever existed.

"Tia?" Dad said from the other side of the bathroom door. "Are you okay?"

It was so unfair. I was ashamed to admit that I didn't want to be anybody's witness—the murderer's or the victim's. I only wanted to be left alone to forget and go back to who I was before, not the coward I had become.

"Yeah, um," I said, through my tears. "I was just messing around."

It was all too much, but I couldn't allow myself to hate the dead and the living for what they had done to me, because I had been a part of it too.

# Chapter Seventeen

I wasn't sure the bath had worked. I didn't feel any different, so I decided to go back to the botanica the next day to see what else Celia could give me. Desperation, according to Dad, made me a prime customer. There were hundreds of potions and trinkets to choose from; there had to be something more powerful.

I joined Mom and Dad in the kitchen, where they were making a snack, kissed them goodnight, and hugged them extra tight.

Instead of closing my bedroom door completely, like I'd done since I was seven, I left it wide open. I even stuffed a flip-flop in the space between the floor and the bottom of the door to make sure it'd stay that way. I was afraid to sleep for fear of what I might dream.

The soft blue glow from the television in the living room should've soothed me like it always had, but I needed more. I had to keep my brain occupied every minute, because if I didn't, I'd be reminded of how the killer took Jonathan and could take me and my family at any moment too.

I wondered what kind of fake scenarios the kids at survival camp dealt with. Had they succeeded? Would I?

Falling asleep seemed impossible. I even tried my go-to trick for sleep, the same one I used whenever I couldn't relax. The one I'd never say out loud. I thought about Julius and what it would be like to kiss him. I'd never kissed anyone before, and as far as I knew, neither had he. Like always, it calmed me, and after a while, I thought about the past New Year's Eve and how we watched the huge twinkling ball as it dropped in Times Square on TV. We watched as frozen celebrities celebrated on the New York City stage. When Gram had had enough, she muted the television and blasted her favorite singer, Tito Puente, from Dad's wireless speakers. It had always thrilled Gram that she and her favorite singer shared the same birthday, April 20.

After only a couple notes of music, Gram pulled me to the middle of the living room floor. I didn't want to dance, even though something inside me begged to. I tried to wiggle out of Gram's grasp, but she wouldn't have it.

"This is part of who you are, *mi amor*," Gram said, then twirled me like a professional salsa dancer.

The congas thumped their way into my blood and soon I couldn't resist. It was almost like an invisible string tugged at my hips and feet. I mimicked Gram as best as I could. I shook my shoulders and moved my feet to the beat. Mom and Dad clapped and soon joined us. We danced until 2:00 a.m., but I hadn't been the least bit sleepy.

Gram bunked with me that night, and once she hit the bed, she was out like a light. I listened to her gentle snore and waited for sleep. But the music still had control of my mind and it took a long time to quiet.

I stared at the ceiling and wished I could feel as happy and safe as I did on New Year's Eve. Instead, I began to sweat, so I got out of bed and turned on the ceiling fan. That's when I realized I had been shaking. My legs gave out and I immediately collapsed onto my purple shag rug.

The room began to spin and soon I felt like someone had placed a hood of terrible fear over my head. My heart began to beat faster than ever, and I thought for sure I would die. Instead of calling out to my parents for help, I silently curled into a ball. Even the thought of Julius didn't help.

When I had calmed down, I climbed back into bed and fell into one of those deep, paralyzing sleeps where the world falls out from beneath you. Those were the kinds of sleeps that really worried me. Anything could've happened while I was unconscious and vulnerable.

In my dream, I stood at a small sink in a foggy bathroom. I glanced into the mirror, but it wasn't my refection I saw. Instead, piercing blue eyes met my gaze. I recognized Jonathan from the photos at the memorial. Only in those, he was smiling. He'd been happy and proud. Even through the haze, I knew he was none of those things in the mirror. He seemed enraged. Willing to do anything to anyone.

Jonathan's chin angled slightly downward as he watched me with more of the whites of his eyes showing than seemed normal. The upper part of his forehead, near the hairline, had become detached from the rest of his face. Gray flesh tinged with pink exposed shiny white bone.

"I'm sorry!" I said.

When Jonathan's stiff hand reached through the mirror and touched the beaded necklaces that hung around my neck, I struggled to wake up, but couldn't. It was like I wore a jacket filled with lead bricks.

Jonathan inhaled deeply, then puckered his pale, cracked lips. He blew black dust into my face. My eyes burned.

Finally, I managed to break free from the invisible weight. I stumbled backward, away from the sink, only to trip over Julius, who stood too close. He tried to tell me something, but a piece of silver tape that stretched across his mouth allowed only grunts. Julius's hands were in metal handcuffs and hung in front of him like two useless tentacles.

Next, Gram and Celia sat in the botanica and wept over something written in yellow chalk above an open window. White curtains danced wildly against a gusty wind. That's when I began to cry too. I'd never seen Gram cry in real life.

Just as I made my way to where Gram stood, she turned away, which crushed me.

Gram shunning me felt like a slap in the face and worked like one too, because I finally woke up. It was early morning and already the warm sun had begun to peek through the curtains. My eyes were irritated and itchy but once I started to rub them, I realized that was a serious mistake. My lids began to swell and felt too heavy for my face.

That wasn't the worst of it. Wheezing had also taken up

valuable space in my chest. It was like someone had taken a tight hold of my lungs, preventing me from taking any deep breaths. But I'd learned my lesson the night of the murder and begun keeping my inhaler tucked safely inside the drawer of my night table. I had to make sure I'd never fumble around for it again.

After I'd used my inhaler, I dragged myself out of bed to see what the deal was with my eyes. Crusty yellow stuff gathered at the corners of my eyes and stuck to my lashes. The whites of my eyes were an angry pink.

It only took a few seconds as I stood at the mirror to re-member my nightmare and how Jonathan blew black dust into my face.

But it was a *dream,* and dreams don't force their way into real life. They can't, that's just how it goes.

Usually.

"Looks a little like pink eye," Mom said, taking a break from buttering warm toast. Then she led me to the couch, where she placed a cool washcloth over each eye. "But, I'm not sure."

"I was fine yesterday."

"Hmm, do you remember anything getting into your eyes?" Mom said.

Did death count? I had no idea, really. What if when you witnessed bad things, a crumb of each one slipped its way into your eyes, or soul, and once they built up, you'd die too?

I shuddered. "I don't know."

"A piece of dirt maybe?"

My brain wanted me to tell Mom everything and fly into

her arms, where safety had always been. But my shoulders simply shrugged in silent betrayal.

Mom made a phone call. "Gram has something that'll help. She's on her way over."

Even though Gram shopping at the botanica embarrassed me, I couldn't deny that she always had a way to fix things. At least, that had been true in the past. But, like the rest of us, Gram had been powerless against a murderer.

After breakfast, Mom sat on the couch and snuggled up to me. I couldn't see her face, but I knew what was coming. "Tia, are you okay?"

The definition of *okay* no longer meant anything to me. The word had simply disappeared from my life, and I was afraid it would never find its way back.

"Yes," I said, which was weird because normally I would've answered with "yeah." *Yes* felt formal and stiff, but Mom didn't catch on.

I rested my head on Mom's lap and thought about telling. I imagined how good it'd feel to shine a light on the monster that had taken over my life and ended Jonathan's. I wanted it gone more than anything, so I allowed the words to rise inside my throat.

"Mom," I croaked.

My heart thudded as Mom patiently waited for me to continue, but when I opened my mouth again, Dad's warning snapped it closed. The same thing could happen to us. I just couldn't put my family at risk.

"If I feel better tomorrow," I said after a minute, "maybe I'll go to the library to see if they need help."

I closed my eyes, which had begun to feel gritty. I wanted to sleep and not wake up until the killer was found.

"Sounds good," Mom said.

"I love you, Mom."

Mom kissed my head. "Love you too, baby."

I felt her watching me and knew she'd resume the questioning, so I fake snored and pretended to sleep. It worked, because she didn't say another word.

Mom gently smoothed my hair, and it didn't take long for me to pass out for real, and when I woke up, she was gone.

Instead, I awoke to find someone else sitting on the other end of the couch. It was a strange, dark figure, and my feet rested on their lap. I'm not sure if it was because my eyes were still irritated and had made my vision wonky, but I jumped off the couch like it had turned into a bed of knives and ran toward the front door.

Gram shot up too. "*Que pasó*? What happened?"

It had been Gram all along.

Mom heard the commotion and ran in from the kitchen. "Is everything all right?"

When I didn't answer, Mom rushed to my side. "Tia, what's going on?"

I didn't know how to answer, because I had no idea what I was doing. I knew what I felt though, and that was the crazy-desperate need to escape.

Mom walked me back into the living room where I avoided Gram's questioning gaze.

"Sorry, just a bad dream," I lied from Dad's favorite chair.

"*Pobre bebé*, poor baby," Gram said. "I don't have anything for that with me, but good news! I got something from Celia that'll fix those poor eyes of yours."

"It's too late to fix what's wrong with my eyes," I blurted.

"Oh? Tell me why that is, *mi amor*," Gram soothed. "Your *abuela* can fix many things."

I tightened my jaw and remained quiet.

"You're starting to worry me, Tia," Mom said. "First you changed your mind about camp—"

"Why are you bugging me?" I had to force an attitude, make her the enemy if I wanted things to stay hidden away. I sprang from the chair and caused it to crash into the wall behind me. "Just leave me alone."

Mom's nose got red right away, which meant she was about to cry, and I felt terrible.

"Tia!" Mom said, her tears disappearing almost as fast as they'd appeared. "Watch yourself!"

Mom dashed to where I stood, and I saw in her eyes what I'd never seen before—sadness and hurt that I'd caused. I was disgusted with myself. I'd never given my parents any kind of trouble, and I hadn't been grounded in a long time, unlike Julius. To be fair, though, his mom and dad were perfectionists and threw punishment around like confetti.

"Go to your room," Mom said. "Now!"

I almost flung myself into Mom's arms and begged for forgiveness, but instead I did what I was told.

# Chapter Eighteen

Even though the ceiling fan spun on high, my room was warm. I pushed open the window as far as it could go and removed the screen, hoping to capture a breeze. Across the street, Marco checked his bike tire.

He grinned large. "Hi, Tia," he said.

I couldn't pretend not to see him again, so I gave a limp wave in return.

People were out and about. Some made their way home from the bus stop down the block, others simply strolled along, enjoying the warm, sunny day. A few had young kids in tow, most likely on their way to the afternoon session at All About Kids, the local daycare center that offered special Saturday classes. Each week was something different. Things like etiquette, sculpting, and painting were big hits. That day, the kids wore karate uniforms.

Most of the families in our neighborhood sent their kids there at one time or another. The center had been around my whole life, and even though it only served kids from ages five through ten, everyone credited it with making genius kids, and sometimes the waiting list hit triple digits.

Some of the success stories were insane. Like this one

eight-year-old kid who did the Heimlich maneuver on his grandfather. Just two weeks before, the school had taught the students what to do in case of a medical emergency. It seemed impossible that an eight-year-old had been skilled enough to squeeze part of a pecan from an adult's esophagus, but that's exactly what happened. My parents never enrolled me in All About Kids, but I wished they had. Then maybe my brain would've been better equipped and I could've saved Jonathan's life. Instead, I silently watched him die.

Just when I was about to step away from the window, a man jogged toward my house. It was a normal sight most of the year, and especially in the summer since Cat Park wasn't too far away. Joggers beat paths all over that place, transforming parts of the grass into hard, dry trails.

As the jogger neared, I noticed he was different. He wore jeans and a dark-gray hoodie. Runners usually wore shorts and tees in the summer.

Instantly, I dropped to my knees and banged my chin on the windowsill so hard on the way down, my teeth clinked. The world around me grew farther and farther away, as if I peered through the wrong end of binoculars. Everything seemed tiny and unreachable. Nothing appeared real, not even me.

Maybe the hooded man was the killer leaving another warning. I stretched through the open window as much as I could without falling out. Maybe if I could tell him that I'd keep his secret, he would never remind me ever again.

But Gram stopped me just before I opened my mouth. "What're you doing, *mija?*"

I didn't hear her come in, and her voice scared me almost as much as the jogger.

"Nothing!" I said, alerting the neighborhood and the running man, who had just caught up with his wife and daughter.

Keeping something so big and horrible hidden inside was hard work, and I was afraid I was starting to crack under the pressure. I tried to hold it together, to pretend life was normal and that I was fine, but the truth continued to search for an opening. Like smoke from a fire, it wanted out.

Gram closed the door behind her. "You may say nothing," she said. "But there's something, and it's only a matter of time before I figure it all out. So why not tell me now?"

I stayed on guard at the window. "There isn't anything to figure out. You just surprised me. That's all."

The bed squeaked under Gram's weight. "I'm talking about more than what just happened."

I blinked back the tears that threatened to give away my lie. "I'm telling you the truth."

Gram was silent for a long time and I wished I knew what she was thinking. "Come," she said finally, "let me put this on your eyelids."

I dragged myself to where Gram patted the bed beside her. "Ugh, is that from the botanica?"

"Of course. Why?"

"How come you don't shop at the other stores like everyone else? Like normal people?" I said.

At first Gram looked hurt, but then she brightened. "I've

always gotten what we need from there and it's never been a problem."

As far as she knew, it hadn't been, but she didn't know about the boat trip and "Priestess Junior."

Gram had just finished coating my irritated lids with something that felt cool and smelled like beets when there was a light knock on my door.

"Come in," I said.

Julius stepped inside. "What happened to you?"

"Not sure, maybe pink eye," I said, happy for the interruption.

My eyes were open just barely enough to see him move in for a better look. It was a little weird, and even though I knew I must've looked a mess, I wasn't self-conscious. Julius had seen me with chicken pox, the stomach flu, and a rash I got from a no-frills laundry detergent Dad bought at the dollar store.

"Yes, it most likely is," Gram said.

I had hoped Gram was right. It was dumb and unrealistic, I knew, but that didn't stop me from thinking about Jonathan and my dream. Had he truly defied the life-and-death rule, the one that said no second chances, just to infect me with who knows what? I shook it off.

Mom stood in the doorway. "I don't think it's anything to worry about," she said. "But let's take a trip to Dr. Bazaz's office and have him take a look."

I returned Mom's gaze, but it was hard. I hated how I'd treated her earlier. "Let's see what Dad says when he gets home, okay?" I said, not wanting to take the long bus ride.

"All right, but he's playing racquetball with some of the

guys after work. In the meantime, I'll call Mrs. Pérez and ask her to come over to see what she thinks, just in case."

Julius and I spoke at the same time. "Mrs. Pérez?"

"She's, like, the janitor in the ER," Julius finished.

"That's what she does here," Mom said, "in this country. But in her country, she was a physician's assistant at one of the best hospitals. Her English isn't good enough to pass testing here in order to get back into her field, but she's working on it."

In my book, that made Mrs. Pérez smarter than the ladies who gave her a hard time outside my window, and I was glad.

"Mom?" I said. "I'm sorry for how I acted earlier."

She smoothed my wiry hair, tucked what she could behind my ear, and kissed my cheek. "I forgive you. I know it's been kind of hard around here with all that's happened, so I'll give you a pass this time."

Then Mom left, and when she got back two minutes later, she held my cell phone. "Don't make me regret this, okay?" She handed it to me.

"Thanks, Mom. I won't."

Gram winked at me but didn't say a word.

Just when we'd finished up lunch, Mrs. Pérez rang the doorbell. Julius, who stayed to eat because his parents were out at their weekly dance lesson, let her in.

Mrs. Pérez wore a stethoscope around her neck. I thought she was probably trying to impress us, but I couldn't say that I blamed her. If I had to clean dirty hospital rooms when I was actually qualified to help the patients, I'd want to show off too.

"*Hola!*" Mrs. Pérez said cheerfully.

We all greeted her. Then Mom offered her something to eat.

Mrs. Pérez placed a large, worn, brown-leather bag on the counter. "Oh, no, thank you," she said. "Last night, Miquel made *arroz con gandules*, plantains, and fried pork chops, and I had the leftovers for lunch. It was *delicioso!*"

Miquel was Mrs. Pérez's oldest son. He was a senior in high school and had just gotten accepted into Boston College on a major scholarship. Probably another reason why some of the neighborhood ladies had issues with her. Gram always told me that jealousy made people ugly on the inside and eventually that ugliness prevented good things from happening in their lives.

"You've taught him well," Gram said.

Mrs. Pérez stood taller and smiled, showing off almost every single tooth in her mouth. "*Gracias.*"

"Thanks for coming over, Carmella," Mom said.

Mrs. Pérez noisily popped on a pair of blue rubber gloves. "I'm happy to help," she said, then gently pulled on each of my lower eyelids.

After she removed a small flashlight from her bag, Mrs. Pérez asked me to look up, down, and everywhere while she shined the light into my eyes. "Does this hurt?" she said.

"No."

"It does look like conjunctivitis," Mrs. Pérez said, using the official term for pink eye.

Mrs. Pérez scraped at the yellow crust around my eyes with her fingernail. It was gross and I bet she was glad she wore gloves.

"This kind of conjunctivitis is like the common cold. It's basically contracted the same way, too, and should pass within a day or two. Nothing serious to worry about."

That was the moment I remembered the elephant pee. The little bottle Celia gave me. My bath. The smell. The dark yellow potion I had soaked my body in.

Maybe Mrs. Pérez had it all wrong.

# Chapter Nineteen

My ears burned with the kind of heat that warms your belly after you realize you've done something wrong and there is no way to fix it.

I don't know how I could've been so stupid. Things like the liquid inside that little bottle should've gone through government testing or something. As a matter of fact, everything the botanica sold should have. And that included whatever Celia had put on my eyelids. Dad had been saying that exact thing my entire life. The liquid was a mystery, and who knew if it could've caused blindness?

"I need my inhaler," I said, then quickly escaped into the bathroom.

For once, I was lying about my asthma, but instead, I felt really dizzy, and I wasn't sure which was worse.

Shakily, I sat on the cool tile floor and thought about getting rid of the bottle Celia gave me. If Dad had ever found out I had used something from the botanica, he'd flip out, especially if it ate away at my eyesight. Maybe I deserved to go blind. What good was having sight if you weren't willing to use it to save a life? To save someone's son, brother, uncle, friend? And what about Mr. Butler? I could've saved him so much heartbreak and sadness, but I chose not to. I was so ashamed and knew I deserved to pay a huge price for my selfishness.

Right away I learned that when I cried it only made my eyes worse, but so did trying to hold the tears back. The only thing that helped was when I splashed cold water on my face. I gulped some, too, and that seemed to help with the dizziness.

I began to search for the bottle but couldn't remember where I had hidden it. I looked everywhere and even shoved the gross toilet-bowl brush to the side, but it wasn't there, or anywhere. It had disappeared.

Just when I gave up looking, there was a knock on the bathroom door. "You coming out, T?" Julius said.

I opened the door and pulled him inside. "I need your help."

"Oh . . . ," Julius blurted, like someone poked him with a pointed stick. "Your eyes," he said. He creeped closer to get a better look. "They're worse. You need to see the doctor."

I sat on the floor with my back against the door. "My eyes are the least of my worries."

Julius took a seat on the edge of the bathtub. "What're you talking about?"

"I have to tell you something. Something big. But first you have to swear on Pop-Pop Isaac that you won't tell anybody."

Pop-Pop taught Julius everything from how to tie a tie to how to make a good tent fort out of bedsheets. Julius loved him more than anything, so I knew he'd keep my secret.

"You know I can't do that, Tia. I don't want to be struck down by lightning or something worse for swearing on Pop-Pop like that."

"Come on, Julius," I whined. "I really need you."

"This better be good, Tia," Julius said after a minute. "I swear."

"Okay, don't freak out or anything, but"—I took a deep breath—"Celia gave me something to put in my bath," I said.

"Who's Celia?"

"The old lady from the botanica?"

"Oh, right," Julius said. "Is it like, bubble bath?"

I yanked on a string that hung from the bottom of my shorts. "Not exactly," I said. "It was a weird yellow liquid, and I'm afraid that might've been what messed up my eyes."

"What? Are you kidding?" Julius said. "Man, Tia, I told you they were freaks. Let's read the ingredients; where's the bottle?"

"That's the thing. I can't find it, but even if I could, there's no label on it. It's just a small, plain-brown bottle."

"Don't worry, we can figure this out." Julius settled into the small space beside me and folded my hand into both of his. I tightened my fingers and never wanted to let go. "It's probably just herbs. Let's ask Gram if she has any idea which ones they might be. She knows everything there is to know about this stuff."

"No way. She'd have to tell my dad and he'll probably flip."

"Okay, then tell me what the stuff is used for," Julius said. "Maybe we can search the internet for some info."

I knew we wouldn't find anything online, but I didn't know how to break it to him.

Julius knew all my secrets and I wanted to tell him this one, too, but something inside me fought to keep it locked up. My mouth transformed into cement and I turned away.

"Don't you trust me?" Julius said, hurt.

It was all too big to handle alone, I knew that. I also knew I needed him, and I began to crack. "It's for . . ."

"Yeah, for what?"

"Protection," I finished.

Julius cocked his head to the side. "Huh?"

"Protection for my family and me—"

"Wait, did somebody threaten you, Tia?" Julius hopped to his feet in a hurry. His eyes were wide and serious. "Who do you need protection from?"

I squeezed his hand, then stood. "It's not just for me, for you too," I finished softly.

"Me? What do you mean?" Julius said.

My throat constricted and made the words tinier and tinier until they disappeared before they made a sound. It was like they refused to put me—to put us—at risk.

We stared at each other for a minute before Julius pulled me into a hug. "It's okay," he said, "whatever it is."

I buried my face in his chest and inhaled his sandalwood body spray. After I had my fill, I began.

"The night of the murder, I couldn't sleep because my asthma was bothering me," I said. "I couldn't find my inhaler right away, but after a few minutes, I found it on the floor near the window, and that's when . . ."

The words shriveled inside my throat again, and tears flowed furiously. Soon, the front of Julius's shirt was wet.

Julius managed to keep his voice calm, but the pounding of his heart against my cheek gave him away. "It's okay, T. Just say it."

"I saw the man, I mean Jonathan, lying on the ground. There was so much blood, too much."

Julius jerked like he'd been electrocuted. "Wait, what're you saying?"

"I saw the killer too. He was holding a knife." I pulled away so that I could see Julius's face. "And he was kneeling over Jonathan."

"WHAT? You have to tell somebody."

"I can't, he told me not to. I mean, not with words, but with the way he looked at me and pointed the knife. He's been leaving me reminders, and I think I might've seen him outside the botanica. He was watching me, then—." I was on the verge of losing it. But after a second, I continued. "There was a weird guy in Mr. Butler's hallway, and who knows? It could've been him too."

I took a deep breath and thought about how the killer could be just about anywhere at any time.

Julius swiped the palm of his hand down his face. "This is insane."

I told him about the warnings, and why I went so willingly behind the curtain with Celia.

"I don't think anyone, or anything, from the botanica can protect us from a murderer," Julius said. "Maybe we should write an anonymous note to Detective Erickson? It's his job to protect people, not the botanica's."

It was a perfectly good idea for actors in a movie, but we weren't in a movie. We were talking about our lives.

"What good would that do? They'd need hard proof, like talking to a witness."

"Yeah, you're right," Julius said, defeated. "Is this the real reason you're not going to camp?"

I nodded. "The last place I want to be in is a cabin in the woods. Plus, I have to protect my family."

"I knew something had to be up," Julius said. "You've been wanting to go since forever."

"Tia?" Mom called from the living room.

I hastily filled Julius in on my plan. It was weak, but it was all I had. "I want to give the liquid one more chance before we do anything, but you have to help me find it first, okay?"

"No way. That's crazy."

"Which part? The liquid, or helping me?"

"The liquid!" Julius said.

I hadn't been happy with it either, but there weren't many choices. "I won't let it anywhere near my eyes this time. And if it doesn't work, I promise we'll do it your way and get a note to Erickson somehow."

"Tia!" Mom called again. I could tell she had run out of patience.

At the sound of Mom's voice, Julius rushed into agreement. "Deal," he said.

We hugged for as long as we could before Mom called again, and for those few minutes, I was safe.

# Chapter Twenty

When we got back to the living room, Mrs. Pérez was gone, and Gram had started dinner. It smelled delicious.

Mom looked up from the pile of dirty clothes she had sorted on the kitchen floor. "You all right?" she said.

"Hmm?" I said, still thinking about where the bottle could be.

Mom straightened. "Your eyes, they feel any better?"

"Oh, a little."

"That's good," Mom said, as she heaped dirty towels into the washer. "Mrs. Pérez said since it's a mild case of pink eye, it should be gone in a couple of days."

"Mild?" Julius said, his own eyes nearly bugging out of his head. He pointed toward me. "That's mild?"

"Yes," Mom said, "but if it was the bacterial kind, you'd need medication. The only thing you need, Tia, is a cold compress. Mrs. Pérez said she'll stop by again later to check in on you, though."

"Humph, a cold compress?" Gram said from her chair at the kitchen table where she was chopping garlic. "That won't get the job done alone." She motioned toward us with her pinky.

It seemed like Mom wanted to say something but held back.

She never disagreed with Gram, at least not openly. I knew she talked to Dad about certain things in private though. When I was ten, I overheard Mom having a conniption after Gram announced she wanted to send me to Puerto Rico for a month so I could get to know my relatives. Needless to say, I never went. Apparently, the conniption didn't just belong to Mom, it was Dad's too. There was no way they were going to send me alone. To be honest, I didn't want to live with complete strangers, even if they were my cousins. We all know relatives can be weirdos, too. Plus, I didn't speak Spanish, which meant it would have been like living in solitary confinement for a whole month.

Gram kissed my forehead. "I've applied something much better than a cold compress or anything you can buy elsewhere."

I knew she meant the stuff she'd put on my eyelids earlier, and I felt unworthy of her kiss since I'd hurt her feelings.

"Don't you worry, my Tia," Gram said. "Your *abuela* always knows what she's doing."

"You shouldn't get so close," Mom said. "It's contagious."

Julius stepped backward. "Uh-oh."

"Too late for you, Jul," I said, thinking about how close I'd been to him.

Gram waved her hand in the air, "Oh, I'll be fine." With that came a slew of kisses for me, then Julius, which made us giggle like little kids. Even Mom cracked a smile.

I watched Gram as she prepared what looked like a feast. *Ensalada de aguacate* already sat in a large bowl. The green of the avocado and the sliced tomato and red pepper looked like

Christmas. I wasn't crazy about avocado salad because there's lime juice in it, but it's one of Dad's favorites. I peeked into a large foil pan just before Gram slid it into the hot oven. It was *pastelón*, my favorite. The only way to explain this dish is that it's a Puerto Rican version of lasagna, only instead of using pasta, we used sweet plantains. Along with being sweet, it's spicy and cheesy and totally delicious. A large loaf of Italian bread lay sliced open on a cutting board. It waited to be transformed into Gram's special garlic bread.

Julius sniffed the air. "All this food is making my stomach do backflips."

Gram patted his shoulder. "Oh, *mijito*, I'll feed you soon enough, but tell me, when are you not hungry?"

Julius smiled big and I couldn't tell if it had been because Gram affectionately referred to him as "little son," something she'd called him on and off for years, or because a tasty meal would soon be coming his way.

Gram handed me a cup of melted butter and a small baking brush. "First cover every inch of the bread with this. Then sprinkle a generous amount of each." Still holding a knife, she pointed to four small bowls, each one filled with salt, grated cheese, fresh chopped parsley, or tiny pieces of garlic.

I didn't hear anything she said after that. I had been too busy feeling like someone had shoved me hard against a wall. My breath pushed out of me, and I struggled for another. The knife Gram held had been well-used in my house. Gram even referred to it as her favorite and insisted on using it whenever she did anything that involved slicing, chopping, or cutting. I never gave the knife a second thought, but now watching Gram move it through the air seemed to control my every heartbeat. It was like we were connected by an invisible thread. The blade seemed shinier and appeared even more razor sharp. I wondered just how far it would have to be plunged into someone's flesh to pierce a vital organ. Would the heart be protected by the rib cage?

Julius rushed to my side. "You okay?" he whispered as he picked up the baking brush off the floor. I didn't even know I had dropped it.

At the sink, Julius kept an eye on me while he washed the brush. It felt odd knowing that I'd done something without realizing it, even if it had been something as small as dropping the brush. I had always thought your body needed permission from your brain to do anything.

"Uh, yeah," I said, then changed the subject. "Why're you cooking such a big dinner?"

"Because your father is bringing Sal home after they play the racquet game."

Julius imitated hitting a ball with a racquet. "It's racquetball, Gram. That's what the game is called."

"Eh"—Gram shrugged—"same thing."

"Since when does Dad have a new friend?" I said. "He's never mentioned Sal before."

Mom added the laundry detergent to the washing machine. "Thank goodness there's no time limit for making friends," she said. "Besides, Sal is pretty new at Dad's job, and Dad wants him to feel comfortable."

After I dressed the bread in garlicky goodness, Julius placed it into the oven on the rack below the *pastelón*.

While Mom searched the cabinet for the iced-tea mix, I sat in one of the kitchen chairs and watched as Gram's apron swayed as she moved across the kitchen with purpose. The killer didn't need to warn me again. The thought of Gram getting hurt was enough for me to keep my mouth shut.

When no one was looking, Julius pointed to Mom and mouthed, *Ask her about the bottle*. I shook my head. There was no way I could do that without having to explain what the bottle was for and why I needed it.

"Is it okay for me and Julius to eat in my room?" I said as I began to set the table. "I'm embarrassed for Dad's friend to see me like this. I look so weird." It wasn't exactly a lie, but I needed an excuse to search for the bottle. I didn't want another episode, or whatever it was that Gram's knife had triggered, to happen again. I knew the bottle couldn't have gotten too far.

Mom moved closer and inspected my eyes. "They're looking a little better, I think. How do they feel?"

"Not so bad," I said.

"Well, as long as you promise to clean up after yourselves, rug included, I guess it'll be okay."

"Promise!" I tugged Julius from his chair and headed for my bedroom. "Call us when dinner is ready, okay?"

"Remember, not even a single crumb is to be left in there. I don't want bugs thinking they can eat at the Lugos' on a permanent basis." Mom had a serious case of bug-a-phobia that stemmed from when she was about my age.

"Okay," I said from the top of the staircase.

———————

After I placed my phone back inside my sock drawer, I got to work right away. I thought maybe the bottle had fallen into the wasteland behind my dresser, which Dad called the "Lost City of Dust." With all my might, I tried to move the dresser away from the wall, but it wouldn't budge.

"Tia?"

I tried again but still no movement, not even half an inch.

"Tia?"

Again, I pushed.

Julius stood behind me. "TIA!"

I turned and faced him. "What?"

"We have to talk about the murder. You're a witness, and there's no magic potion for that. You have to tell Detective Erickson exactly what you saw."

Even though I'd been mortified by the fact that Gram had shopped at the botanica, I refused to believe that she'd been wrong about it all these years. Or worse, crazy.

"I can't, he knows where I live. Where *we* live."

"Erickson will protect us," Julius said.

"How can you say that? Or better yet, how can you trust him to do that if he's not even smart enough to figure out who killed the guy? Erickson's a joke. I don't care about him or anyone else." I gulped a mouthful of air and almost swallowed the terrible words that fought their way out, but failed. "I don't even care about Jonathan," I finished.

It was the last lie that hurt the most and caused burning behind my eyes. I did care about Jonathan, but I didn't want to. I didn't want to be responsible for giving a dead man peace or for protecting the public from some freaking murdering maniac. I didn't want to feel guilty. Why hadn't Erickson been smarter? Why couldn't he work harder and find the killer? It wasn't fair. I felt like someone had turned me upside down and caused every emotion and feeling to become mixed up and confused. Why was I such a coward?

"Tia," Julius said, "that's crazy and I know you don't mean it."

Tears escaped down my cheeks and soon I was bawling against Julius's chest, again. I was so tired of crying but couldn't seem to stop.

"You have to tell everything, Tia. Even about the warnings. But don't worry, you don't have to do it alone," Julius said. "I'm going with you."

His voice was gentle and sweet, and it lulled me, if only for a minute, from thoughts about the murder, the lost bottle, Erickson, and my selfish, terrible self.

# Chapter Twenty-One

We sat for what was left of the afternoon, each in our own thoughts. When Gram called out from the kitchen that dinner was ready, Julius said, "I'll get it and bring it back."

I sat on my bed and battled the voices inside my head that told me Julius was right about talking to Erickson.

"Delivery," Julius said, using his knee to push open the door. He carried our plates of food and suddenly, as if my stomach had grown eyes of its own, I was starved.

I cleared a spot on the floor by my closet, and it was a good thing the door was closed, or Julius might have lost his appetite. My closet looked like a small explosion had gone off inside. It probably wouldn't have been too much of a surprise based on the condition of my bedroom though. Instead of an organized storage place for clothes and shoes, my closet had been a tomb for old stuff I had no idea what to do with. Inside were all my old notebooks; a robe slathered in fake blood I'd worn on Halloween as a zombie wizard; two pairs of rain boots, one leaky and one so ugly I'd never wear them in public; and an untold amount of outgrown dresses I couldn't stand to part with. Add to all of that some various papers, games, puzzles, and dust, and you had an on-point description.

We sat down on the carpet in silence. It felt like words floated between us, waiting to be said, but what words? What were you supposed to say to somebody after you've admitted you're a terrible human being and said you didn't care about other humans, even if it wasn't true?

We ate in seven minutes flat. Julius marked it with a loud burp. "Excuse me," he said.

While we stacked our dishes and searched for crumbs in the fibers of the carpet like Mom commanded, Dad came home.

"I whipped your butt today, Alex," said an unfamiliar voice. It was friendly and on the verge of a laugh.

"Yeah," Dad said. "I'll get you next time, Sal. You can count on it."

"We'll see, old man. Want to go again tomorrow? If you're not in too much pain, that is."

"Nah, tomorrow's Sunday. Family day around here."

"Cool," Sal said.

After Julius placed our dishes on the stack of library books that sat on the floor nearby, he said, "While we're down here, may as well look for the bottle." Then he crept beneath my bed. I hoped he wouldn't find anything embarrassing, like underwear.

"You know," Julius continued, "even if we find it, you still have to talk to Erickson."

But I had already made up my mind. I had made my choice, and it was to keep my family safe.

"You know what my dad said right after the murder?" I said.

Julius's skinny legs stuck out from under the bed. He looked like the male version of the Wicked Witch of the East, only there was no house, just my crumpled blanket.

"Whoa, Tia," he said as he began to back out. "What're these doing here?"

Panicked, I began doing a mental scan and tried to account for every pair of undies I owned.

When Julius's almost-six-foot body had cleared the bed frame, he was holding an unopened pack of long-lost Pokémon cards. I felt both completely relieved and totally ridiculous. Even if he had seen my underwear in the junkyard beneath my bed, he wouldn't have announced it. At least I didn't think so.

"I haven't held these babies in like, three years," Julius said. "I thought they were gone forever."

He brushed giant dust balls from his shirt. "Now, what were you saying?"

"I was telling you that right after the murder, when Erickson was questioning everybody, Dad said the killer could come back and hurt anybody who might speak up."

"Then maybe," Julius said thoughtfully, "we could make an anonymous phone call to him."

I knew it wasn't right, but I had been irritated with Julius for not hearing what I said. "No, that's a dumb idea. I can't take any chances. And I don't know why you can't understand that. I'm trying to protect everyone, including you."

"I get it, Tia, but it's not just about us. It's about the guy who lost his life. Lost it, just like"—he snapped his fingers close to my face—"that." Julius shook his head in disgust, and it stung. "How can you ignore something so huge?"

His words may as well have been a million cactus needles. It was painful to watch how his annoyance grew. Julius had always been on my side, and I mourned the fact that he might not ever be again.

I swallowed Julius's disappointment and hoped it could be reversed, if and when Erickson solved this case. I only hoped it wouldn't take too long.

"Julius, just move the dresser!" The order pushed out from me like it had been fueled by gasoline and a match.

Without a word, Julius silently edged the dresser away from the wall.

"Thank you," I said, not even sure he had heard me but thinking it probably wouldn't have mattered anyway.

I waded through old homework sheets, pictures of me and Julius making the craziest faces in a photo booth, two hairbrushes, the MetroCard I thought had gotten stolen at school, four hairbands, and a thick layer of dust. It seemed like the bottle had never existed.

"It's not here! Where the—" I said.

At that moment, Dad tapped lightly on my door. "Tia? Come meet Sal."

I guessed Mom hadn't gotten the chance to tell Dad about my eye situation, because when I opened the door, he flinched at the sight of me. "What happened, honey?" he said.

The smoke from the candle by the front door drifted in past me and settled inside my room. It reminded me of my visit to the botanica. Dad must've blown the flame out, and I wondered if he had also turned the statue around, making the wall the only thing that protected our house.

"Mrs. Pérez thinks it's pink eye." I grabbed a tissue from the box on my desk and dabbed at the wetness of both eyes.

Dad was as puzzled as we had been. "Mrs. Pérez?"

"It's a long story." I tossed the tissue into the trash can, then bathed my hands in blueberry sanitizer. "Can I skip meeting Sal? I look pretty disgusting."

"You'll always look beautiful to me," Dad said, then kissed each temple in typical Dad style. "But I understand."

I thought parents were bound by some weird law that stated you cannot, under any circumstance, tell your daughter the truth about her appearance. There was one instance that proved the rule truly existed, and that was my first-grade school photo. I had been shy and pretty much traumatized by the photographer's assistant, who insisted on combing my curly hair with one of the little black combs they were handing out for free. It didn't matter that I had declined the comb by politely saying "no, thank you." The overeager assistant enthusiastically dove her hand straight into the box of plastic freebies like she was about to hand out Halloween candy and went to town on my head.

The photo shoot was right after lunch and recess, so my hair went from slightly frizzy to light-socket-finger-pointing-Albert-Einstein status with one swipe of a free comb. Like a bunch of ghosts trying to get a message across to the living, every unruly hair on my head rose into the atmosphere, ready to be caught on film as proof that I had attended Mrs. Tracy's first-grade class.

That, combined with a chocolate milk stain in the shape of the state of Texas across the front of my dress, led the photographer to repeatedly look around his lens as though he was trying to see me in real life.

After I had grimaced through the photo and begun walking away, I'd overheard the photographer tell the assistant that she was no hairdresser. The assistant had a laugh over that—and me, I guessed—but the photographer stayed straight-faced. The photo had been a complete mess. I looked like some sideshow kid who'd been found in the wild living among wolves or something. And yet my parents loved that photo like it was a Picasso.

I'm not sure why, but when Dad showered me with the compliment in front of Julius, heat rose from the tips of my polished toenails to the tops of my pierced ears. There, the words sat and burned. I was glad when Mom called Dad to the table before he could do any more damage.

I plopped down on my bed. Julius sat beside me but made sure to keep his distance. I felt guilty about how I had treated him and wanted to apologize, but it was still too early. He'd only think I had changed my mind about the Erickson thing and probably wouldn't stop pushing.

"I'm a prisoner in my room. I can't even search the rest of the house until Dad's friend leaves," I said.

"Pretty sure he doesn't care about what you look like. There are more important things happening in the world, you know," Julius said.

He'd stung me once again.

Without another word, he stood, picked up the dishes, and headed for the door.

I hopped off the bed and blocked his path. "Where're you going?"

His eyes were unreadable and cold. "Home," he said, then pushed by me.

He'd get over it, I told myself and closed the door behind him.

# Chapter Twenty-Two

I put my ear to the door and listened as Gram asked Julius if he was coming back for seconds.

"No, thank you, Gram," Julius said. "Mom wants me home early."

"Oh?" Gram replied in her I-know-you're-lying voice.

Dad introduced Julius to Sal, and they exchanged a few words about how good Gram's food was before Sal went into nosy mode. He asked Julius all kinds of questions. I could tell by Julius's short answers that he wanted to get out of there quickly, and it wasn't too long before I heard his goodbyes and the door closing behind him.

Forks and knives continued to scrape against our good plates, and I hoped the meal was coming to an end. I began to feel like a caged zoo animal.

My heart sank when Gram asked if anyone wanted seconds and Sal jumped on it.

"Yes, thank you. Everything's delicious. Alex, your mother sure can cook."

"*Gracias*," Gram said, a smile in her voice.

"Yeah, thanks to her, I have this."

I didn't have to see Dad to know he patted his belly.

"Sal, do you live alone?" Mom asked.

"No, I have a roommate. The rent is just too high for me to live alone. And even with a roommate, it's still a struggle. It's not what you'd call a nice apartment either, and most nights I can't sleep because my neighbors are so noisy. I go out walking at all hours until I'm so tired, I could sleep through anything."

Polite laughter filled our kitchen, Sal's being the loudest. I really wanted to get a look at him so that I could put a face to how lame he was.

Mom said something I missed, and Sal continued.

"Seriously, I wish my place was as nice as this. What do you have here? Three bedrooms?"

"Two. It's small, especially upstairs with the bedrooms so close to the staircase. If it's noisy down here, you hear every bit of it up there, but we're happy in our little house."

"I'd do anything for a view. Your bedrooms must have a perfect view of the city, right?"

"Well," Dad said, "if we lean out and bend our necks in an uncomfortable position, then yes, the view is nice."

"Oh, don't listen to him," Mom said. "It's not that bad."

"Okay, maybe I'm exaggerating a bit," Dad said.

I took a break from listening at the door and stretched out on my carpet. I hadn't noticed just how tired I'd been. I closed my eyes, which had started to feel better. I had only been lying there for a few minutes when Jonathan's ashen face loomed before me in a dream.

I scrambled to my feet and tried to shake the dream loose, but Jonathan had been tethered to my consciousness. I took a hit of my inhaler and wondered if he'd always haunt my life. I wouldn't have blamed him if he did. I'd do the same thing if I had been the one left to die.

The only good thing about losing a few minutes to a haunted dream was that the meal had finally ended. The dishes clanked and rattled as someone brought them over to the sink.

"So, Alex," Sal said, "does the boss know who's been stealing?"

"Not yet, but he's got plans."

"Really?"

"Yeah, I'm sure we'll find out who the culprit is pretty soon," Dad said.

"Hey, maybe it's that new kid. What's his name? The one who's working for the summer?"

"Who? Big Mike? Nah, I doubt it. He's a little obnoxious, but not a thief."

That explained the red dots on Big Mike's sneakers—cherry juice.

Conversation droned on, and all I thought about was how badly I wanted to search the bathroom again. Just as I cracked open the door to make a run for it, I heard my name. Sal wanted to know where I was.

"Tia's not feeling well today," Gram said. "She's in her room."

"That's too bad, I was really looking forward to meeting her. Anything . . . serious?"

"No, thank God," Mom said. "Just a case of pink eye. We have a doctor friend who's coming by later to check up on her."

"Hmm, I had an aunt who believed weird things about people who got pink eye," Sal said.

"Really?" Mom said. "Like what?"

"Oh, it's just a ridiculous old wives' tale," Sal said. "Nothing to worry about."

"Still, I'd like to know."

Sal laughed stiffly. "It was something about the eyes trying to rid themselves of something."

My hand flew to my mouth and softened a gasp and the choking cough that followed. I crept closer to the staircase as carefully as possible and hoped to get a glimpse of Sal. No luck, though. He was out of my field of vision.

"Like?" Mom said.

"Oh, who knows? I'm sorry I even brought it up."

Gram cleared her throat. "I'm sure your aunt meant well, but—"

Again, Sal chuckled. It lightened the mood downstairs, but upstairs, I was numb. "Yeah, that's how most people react to Aunt Lulu's way of thinking. They usually refer to her as Aunt *Loca*."

Dad snickered.

"Anyway," Gram said, "I've already applied something helpful to Tia's eyelids, so they'll be healed in no time."

"Botanica stuff, Mami? You know how I feel about that," Dad said.

"You don't believe in that stuff, Alex?" Sal said.

"No, and please don't tell me that you do."

"Sure do. Grew up in a house that was heavy into it. We had a candle for every desire in our family."

"Then no offense," Dad said, "but I think those places only give desperate people false hope. People think if they have a health problem, the botanica can cure them. They think if they don't have money to make it through the week, they can light a botanica candle and their pockets will be magically filled with money. It's a scam, plain and simple, and I'm afraid my mother will be hurt by it one day."

"I'm too smart for that, *hijo*," Gram said. "True, some people can get caught up, but—"

"Mom, we shouldn't get into this now. We have company."

"Excuse me, I have to take this call," Sal said, even though I never heard his phone ring. "I'll be right back."

When the muffled buzzing started, I didn't know what it was, but then the familiar rhythm revealed itself. It was a text. I fumbled with the knobs of my dresser drawer, and as I tugged it open, I debated whether or not I wanted to read the message or shut the phone down. Just as I tossed the socks aside, it buzzed again.

*Unknown.*

Blood roared inside my head and filled it with white noise. I tapped out my passcode, took a deep breath, then opened the text. *Just don't tell. It'll be our secret.*

But I had already told Julius. My hands trembled as I deleted the text. When I slid the phone back into the drawer, Sal came back into the room. The coincidence almost dropped me to my knees.

Gram wasted no time asking if he was up for dessert. I knew it was wrong, but my blood chilled at her offering. Had she just fed a killer?

# Chapter Twenty-Three

I cracked open the door and listened. The conversation downstairs hadn't changed. Maybe I was paranoid. Texting and leaving warnings for me to find had been one thing, but walking into my house would be another. So I blew off the text and Sal's absence as a fluke.

I flopped belly first onto my bed, then hung my head off the side, directly in front of the laundry basket, which had been filled with a mound of clean clothes. Something peeked out through a tangle of clean laundry. At first, I wasn't sure what it was but then, all at once, I knew. It was the bottle Celia had given me. I tumbled from the bed in what I could only describe as a floor routine like in a gymnastic competition, except I wasn't as controlled or elegant. But I had rolled, scooped, jumped, and scored a perfect ten in my book.

Just as I began walking toward the bathroom for my bath, the doorbell rang. Mrs. Pérez was back. "I have drops for Tia," she said.

"Thank you so much," Mom said.

Dad introduced Mrs. Pérez to Sal, then Mom made her way to me.

Instead of going into the bathroom, I turned around and

hurried back into my room. Once inside, I slipped the bottle underneath a pillow just in time for Mom to enter.

Mom applied a drop to each eye, then went back downstairs.

"Well, I should get going if I want to make the next bus. But first I need to use your bathroom," Sal said.

"Sure," Dad said, "upstairs to the right."

I eased my door closed.

Sal jogged up the staircase, but instead of footsteps going down the hall toward the bathroom, they stopped right outside my door.

I watched as my doorknob slowly turned, and just as I was about to yell out, Dad stopped him before he entered. "No, that's Tia's room. The bathroom is the door to the right."

"My apologies," he said, through the door. Then in a whisper, he added, "So sorry, Tia."

It was another few seconds before he moved on. My entire body crawled with alarm.

After a couple of minutes, the toilet flushed, and Sal made his way to the kitchen, where he said his goodbyes.

"Wait," Gram said. "Don't forget your hood."

There were a few light laughs, then Dad said, "Mom, it's called a hoodie."

"Eh, doesn't matter. You say *hood-ie*, I say hood. We all know what I mean."

More laughter then, but not from me. My lungs instantly reacted to that one sentence even before my brain comprehended the words. My inhaler suddenly felt like a barbell inside my pocket, and when I fished it out, I double puffed. One right after the other, I sucked down the bitter mist.

My mind began to race. But instead of thoughts, they were a collage of gruesome visions. Jonathan lying on the ground, the blood-stained sidewalk, the memorial, the knife, the killer's hand, and poor Mr. Butler.

The killer had worn a hoodie that night.

I sat a minute longer while my lungs eased, then ran to the window to get a glimpse of Sal and his hoodie, but the bus had already pulled away from the stop.

The sun hung low in the sky, and as the bus moved by my house, I was able to see inside. Everything, even the light-blue plastic seats, took on a pink hue. A few teenagers, a man with a bushy beard, and an old woman holding a cane and wearing a purple turban sat scattered throughout the bus. A man carrying a black hoodie walked toward the back of the bus, but it was impossible to get a good look at him.

I broke out of my bedroom prison and headed downstairs.

Mom had just finished clearing the table and Dad was taking out the garbage.

When Dad got back, he held a small ceramic figurine of three monkeys. "Look what I found on our stoop," he said.

Each of the three monkeys held its hands to either its ears, eyes, or mouth. Hear no evil, see no evil, speak no evil. They're known as the three wise monkeys, and the sight of them made me gasp for air even though I had just used my inhaler.

A reminder from Sal.

I clumsily plopped down into a kitchen chair and almost

completely missed it. My legs continued to shake even as I crossed and uncrossed them.

I tucked my quivering hands underneath my thighs. "That was on our stoop?"

"Yeah, there was no one around to claim it. Bad for them, lucky for me," Dad said with a silly grin plastered to his face. "They'll look great on my desk at work."

Dad had all sorts of weird things on his work desk. He loved charm machines and had a collection of tiny robots, elves, elephants, and race cars. Dad always said it was the little things that counted, but he had no idea the monkeys were far from little. They were huge, enormous, massive.

Mom took a closer look. "It's kind of ugly," she said.

It was more than ugly. It terrified me. Even though I wanted to, I couldn't take my eyes off the figurine. Nothing else existed. Not the kitchen walls, the floor, or the chair I sat in. Everything just melted away. The killer had held the figurine in his hands and now Dad had held it too.

"You should throw it into the garbage," I said. "We don't know where it's been, and it's probably loaded with germs."

It was a lame thing to say, but I hoped Mom would agree anyway.

It was enough for Mom to wrinkle her nose, but not enough to ban the figurine. "Put it in the sink," she said. "I'll give them a good scrubbing later."

Dad gently placed the monkeys into the sink. I wished for their heads to simultaneously fall off, but that didn't happen.

"Come on, Tia," Mom said, "let's put in the drops Mrs. Pérez brought over."

Gram got ready to leave, and I could tell the sight of the drops annoyed her. "I'm going to make sure your eyes return to perfect health," she said.

We all knew that meant Gram was headed to the botanica but no one mentioned it.

After Gram left, Mom released the clear liquid into each eye. I was relieved when it didn't burn like the one time when I'd used allergy drops. It had been so bad then, I'd thought for sure I'd lose an eyeball.

"Now go rest and give it a chance to work," Dad said as he kissed both my temples. "Mom and I are off to The Food Dudes. We're out of milk and you know I can't function without my morning coffee."

Dad snorted like he always did every time he or someone else said "The Food Dudes." According to Mom, the grocery store chain started when two hippies, Rodney and Ike, began planting vegetables in their small Bronx backyard. Dad said their thumbs were so green that it was impossible to eat everything they grew, so they set up a table outside their house and started selling produce really cheap. People loved that they could afford fresh vegetables for their families, and they bought out whatever the Dudes offered each weekend. Soon the Dudes rented a small store, and before anyone knew it, they had a few more stores, then a few more, including one in our neighborhood.

I watched from my window as my parents made their way toward the store. Their absence gave me the perfect opportunity to sneak out of the house. The bath would have to wait a little while longer.

It was a long shot, but if there had been some connection between Sal and Jonathan, there was a good chance Mr. Butler would've known.

When my parents were completely out of sight, I hurried back to Pioneer Street, where it seemed to be too quiet for a Saturday evening in the summer. In Brooklyn, summer was usually the busiest and loudest time of the year. But that day, even the handful of kids who hung out on street corners and stoops played quietly. When it came to Pioneer Street, it seemed the world still mourned.

I pressed the buzzer without thinking of what I'd say. I hadn't been expected and for all I knew, Mr. Butler would think I was just plain rude.

Part of me was glad when no one answered, but I couldn't just leave, so I forced myself to ring the bell again. After a couple of seconds, Mr. Butler's husky voice came over the intercom.

"Who's there?" he said.

"It's Tia."

There was some fumbling and static, then all went silent.

"Hello? Are you there?" I said.

Still no answer.

I looked out onto the sidewalk and contemplated what to do next. That's when I spotted the little boy who'd left his stuffed dog for Jonathan. His mom spoke to another woman, and the boy had plopped himself down on the sidewalk, not too far away. He sat so still I wondered if he had fallen asleep, but when he started to rock back and forth, I knew he hadn't. It wasn't long before his mom noticed and scooped him up in a hug. He nestled his face against her neck while she patted his small back. I remembered doing the same thing to Mom when I was sad or scared, or just needed to know everything would be okay.

I pressed the bell again and held it. When I pulled back, the small, round speaker above the buttons crackled.

"I was wondering," I blurted out quickly in case the intercom conked out again. "If we could talk?"

The only noise I could clearly make out was the soft clicking sound the buzzer made as the door unlocked.

# Chapter Twenty-Four

Mr. Butler's apartment door stood slightly ajar. I knocked lightly.

"I hope I'm not bothering you," I said.

"Not at all, come in, come in!"

I pushed the door further open, and, as if on cue, Potato bounded from somewhere deeper inside the apartment. Her tail wagged like crazy and seemed to keep time. *Tick-tock, tick-tock.*

I knelt to greet her just as she rolled onto her back, ready for belly rubs, which I happily gave her.

Potato danced in circles. I laughed and once again felt lighthearted.

"Okay, okay, Potato," Mr. Butler said.

We sat and soon I found myself telling Mr. Butler all about my research and dog drama. He was so easy to talk to that the words just spilled out. "What kind of dog is she?" I asked.

"Oh, I'm guessing a little bit of this and a little bit of that," Mr. Butler said. "Bottom line is, she's the perfect pup for me. Doesn't even shed. I got her from the shelter. Poor thing was found in a puppy mill along with countless others. Jonathan and I nursed Miss Potato here back to health, and when she was strong enough, I adopted her."

Potato hopped onto Mr. Butler's lap, curled up, and closed her eyes. She'd been one lucky dog and it seemed as if she knew it.

"I don't have any brownies for you this time," Mr. Butler said as he scratched behind Potato's ears. "But how about something to drink?"

"No, thank you."

"Okay," Mr. Butler said. "But let me know if you change your mind. And I promise to have rice pudding for you next time."

"That'd be awesome. Thank you."

"So," Mr. Butler said. "To what do we owe this honor?"

I searched my brain for just the right words. "Well, I can't stop thinking about Jonathan." Not only had they been the right words, they were true ones too.

Mr. Butler looked away. "Neither can I."

"When do you think the funeral will be?" I said.

I thought if I could attend, I'd get a good look at who else was there. Though would the murderer really attend his victim's funeral? I doubted it.

"I haven't—" Mr. Butler paused for a few seconds before he finished, "heard of any arrangements yet."

As if Potato knew Mr. Butler was upset, she gave his face a few swipes with her wrinkly tongue.

"Did Jonathan ever mention someone named Sal?"

"No, he never spoke much of anyone," he said. "Why do you ask?"

"Oh, I just—"

Potato hopped down, then disappeared into the kitchen, where she pawed her metal bowl.

"She's a hungry girl," Mr. Butler said. "I'll be right back."

Before Mr. Butler entered the kitchen, I asked if I could use the bathroom.

He pointed toward the hallway behind me. "Sure, it's just back that way."

It was a small apartment and I found the bathroom easily.

Once inside, I noticed a black uniform hanging from a hook on the back of the door. The triangular black-and-gold patch on the arm of the shirt seemed familiar, but no matter how long I stared at it, I couldn't remember why.

"Is everything okay?" Mr. Butler said from the hallway.

"Yes," I said, embarrassed that maybe I took too long.

I washed my hands and when I stepped out, Mr. Butler waited just outside the bathroom door.

Silently, we both made our way back into the kitchen. I played with Potato for a couple of minutes, then said an awkward goodbye. That's when Mr. Butler, unsmiling, blocked my path.

What was he doing? His seriousness freaked me out. Before I could question him, someone knocked on the apartment door. It was Elaine, the woman who had walked Mr. Butler home from the memorial. I said a quick hello to her and left.

I thought about why Mr. Butler had acted so weirdly the whole way home and finally figured maybe he thought I had snooped inside his bathroom cabinets or something. I couldn't blame him. I'd hate it if someone went through my things without asking. What if Mr. Butler wouldn't let me help out with Potato anymore? I sulked for a little while, then decided I'd clear it up when I saw him next.

My pace slowed almost to a stop when I spotted someone sitting on the steps outside my house. I thought maybe Sal had come back and started panicking, but it was only Marco scrolling through his phone. I needed to take another bath and didn't want to waste time talking about new movie theaters or anything else. Luckily, he hadn't seen me and began to walk away.

Once inside I locked up and headed for my bedroom, where I placed the beaded necklaces Celia had given me on the night table. Since Mom and Dad were still out grocery shopping, I went into the bathroom and prepared for my bath. I pinched my nose closed, then poured the thick yellow liquid into the warm, churning bathwater.

Just as the tub filled, our doorbell rang. I figured Marco had come back but I never answered the door when I was home alone, so I ignored it. When it began to ring again and again, I worried that maybe it was important, so I threw on my clothes and ran to the door.

If we lived in an apartment, most likely our door would've had a peephole, but we didn't. I put my ear against the smooth wood just as someone knocked heavily. I froze, terrified. Marco would've never banged on our door like that, at least I didn't think so. Again, I thought about Sal. I hurried to my bedroom where I quickly placed the botanica beads back around my neck and hoped they could make up for the protection of the bath.

I dug out my cell phone from the drawer, intent on dialing 911, but all was quiet again. Maybe it was only an impatient deliveryman with the wrong address? Still, I dialed Mom's number but there was no answer and her voicemail didn't pick up. Neither did Dad's when I called him next. It didn't surprise me, since it happened a few times before. Mobile C, our cell phone carrier, had terrible service.

My next call was to Julius, but he didn't answer either. I thought maybe he was ignoring me because he was still angry, so I dialed his house phone.

"Hello, Mrs. Carson," I said when Julius's mom picked up. "It's Tia. May I please speak to Julius?"

"Hi, honey, how're you?" she said sweetly. "Julius told me you weren't feeling well."

"I'm feeling better, thank you. Is Julius home?" I said. I hoped he wasn't still mad.

"No, he's out with his dad, but they should be back any minute now."

"Okay, would you please ask him to come over as soon as he gets in?"

"Will do," she said.

On my way back to the bathroom, I jumped at a dull thump coming from the back door. Cautiously, I turned back toward the stairs, deciding to follow the sound.

On the staircase, I tucked my cell into my pocket just as it rang. It almost scared me to death.

"Julius?" I said.

"No, it's Mommy. I've been trying to call you, but my phone

isn't working again. I have bad news, Tia." She waited another second before she finished. "We were passing the botanica on our way back from the grocery store and . . . we found out Gram has been rushed to Methodist Hospital. She fainted while shopping."

A burning pain started inside my head, then moved over the rest of my body. It made me feel like I'd been set on fire. When the tears came, they scalded my cheeks.

I forgot all about the noise I'd heard. "What happened?" I howled.

Dad took the phone from Mom. "We're not sure yet, but we'll know soon, honey. We're going to the hospital now."

I ran down the rest of the steps. "I have to see her! Please, come get me."

"No, sweetheart, it's best if you stay home for now. We'll call you as—"

"Dad?"

I thought the connection had been dropped, but it was my battery. It had gone dead.

# Chapter Twenty-Five

Again, the unfamiliar noise. Only this time the thud was louder than the first.

I was too afraid to peek through the window near the back door, but I was determined to make sure the door was locked. I turned the knob clockwise, but it spun roughly out of my hand—in the opposite direction.

A wave of terror scurried across my scalp when a thud rattled the doorframe. I leapt backward.

Someone wanted in. Maybe Sal had come back after all.

The doorway to my house had always brought safety. Until then it had only ever allowed in the good—Dad home from work, Mom bringing my favorite things, Gram with armfuls of love, and Julius. But today, instead of safety, comfort, and love, it brought the worst kind of danger.

Almost immediately, my lungs refused to fully inflate no matter how much air I tried to push into them. I pumped my inhaler and thought about the best place to hide. In the movies, bad guys always searched underneath beds and inside closets, but never . . . the bathtub. So that's where I hid.

Once inside the bathroom, I pushed the door closed. The

broken lock had been the latest addition to Dad's to-do list. Something I had forgotten about when I chose this hiding place.

*CRACK!* went the back door. Then footsteps hurriedly made their way into the kitchen.

I moved a corner of the shower curtain aside, then immersed myself into the warm water. My shirt and shorts filled with air and formed small balloons. I forced my eyes shut and willed myself small against the porcelain tub.

Next, the sound of running feet burst into the quiet of the living room. I held my breath, thankful for the power of my inhaler, and waited for whatever would happen next.

I wished Julius was with me. I knew together we'd get through it, but alone I was doomed.

"Hello?" a man's voice bellowed into the quiet.

My body jerked like I had been jabbed with a sharpened pencil. The water rippled.

A scream began to inch from my throat, like a snake prepared to strike. Slowly it worked its way from its safe haven and into my mouth, but I clenched my teeth and formed an enamel cage. I slipped further into the water, leaving just my face and ears out.

From my safe spot, I listened as a stranger treaded around my living room like he belonged there. Like we were in his house and not mine.

When the stranger sprinted up the steps toward the bedrooms, I froze from fright. Because my bedroom was close to the bathroom, when he flung open my bedroom door it slammed hard against the wall. The shelf above the toilet shook. The small jars of Mom's fancy soaps, Q-tips, and cotton balls rattled in their spots. I imagined Gram's botanica items vibrating inside the cabinet too.

"Tia, we both know this game of hide-and-seek can only go on for so long," the man said.

The voice seemed familiar, but my brain had shut down. I couldn't even tell if it was Sal or not, and I had only heard his voice a couple of hours before.

"Nothing can help you, and for that I'm sorry. You seemed like a nice kid."

If only I had listened to Julius and called Detective Erickson.

If only I had stayed away from my window that night.

If only.

If only.

My asthma kicked up a few notches, and with every new breath, my lungs refused to fully inflate. My inhaler, still burrowed inside the pocket of my shorts, was as wet and as useless as the rest of me.

I began to think about my parents and how they'd grieve for me once I was gone. Would they regret not having any more kids? At least they'd have each other. But what about Gram? If he killed me, it would be like he'd killed two people, because I was sure Gram would stop living if she lost her only granddaughter.

I blinked away the tears that flooded my eyes, freeing them. I needed to see clearly if I hoped to make some sort of survival plan. When I focused on the window above the tub, I knew I had an escape. I'd stand on the edge of the tub for height, then jump out of the window. It was only a few feet to the ground. I would get scraped up for sure, but nothing too serious. If I stayed where I was, death was definite.

But he was too close for me to make any kind of move right now.

"Oh Tia, if only he had stuck to our plan, none of this would've happened," the killer said.

Our plan?

The door to my parents' bedroom squeaked open, and I knew the bathroom would be next.

"But he wouldn't listen to reason," he said.

The voice continued to nag at me, but I still could not place it.

"We couldn't just let Jonathan go around giving people loads of money, even if he was the one who had easy access to it." He sighed like he was sorry, but I knew he couldn't be. "That would've been like having a giant guilty sign pointing directly at us!"

I heard him as he moved around inside my parent's bedroom and felt sick.

"Gawking out onto the street when you should've been asleep was a bad idea, but I guess you know that by now," the stranger said.

My heart hammered against my ribs so hard and fierce I thought for sure he'd hear.

"I tried to warn you. I'm not a total monster, you know."

The killer's cell phone rang. It filled the air with an obnoxious chimpanzee screech. I had no idea how I did it, but

I managed to keep myself still even though the sound almost made me shriek.

"Yeah, what's up?" he said, moving further away. "Hey, would you stop worrying?"

He listened, then sighed.

"Calm down," he said. "I've just got this one loose end to take care of."

Me. I was the loose end.

"Okay, I'll meet you in front of Georgie's Diner at nine o'clock," he said, then ended the call.

That's when I took a deep breath and completely submerged myself.

In my mind the window grew nearer and nearer until freedom was just a few inches in front of me. My arms and legs quaked with fear and anticipation, but in reality, I knew escape was unlikely.

Breathlessness was nothing new to me. Besides getting me out of PE, this was the only gift asthma had ever given me. I knew what it was like to live on half-filled lungs. I knew how to hang on.

Still, my lungs burned and begged to be replenished. I was almost out of air, but still I waited. I desperately needed a miracle.

But before I knew what happened, my hiding spot disappeared. The killer yanked open the shower curtain with such force, the bar fell onto the tiled floor with a loud clank. I shot up into a seated position and choked. In huge gasps, I gulped the air. Bathwater cascaded over the side of the tub in a huge rush. My eyes burned and my hair hung in front of my face. I could not see clearly.

A man hovered above me, bloated veins zigzagging across his forehead, as his dark, bulging eyes took me in.

The man reached into his shirt pocket and took out a napkin from the House of Pizza.

"These always seem to come in handy," he said, then wiped bathwater from his face.

His crooked pinky faced the wrong direction.

Mr. Butler.

And he stood on perfectly healthy legs—not a knee brace in sight.

# Chapter Twenty-Six

I watched in disbelief as Mr. Butler tapped out a rhythm on both thighs. "Don't be so shocked. My knee works just fine." With that, he danced an eerie, slow waltz.

Then he took hold of my arm and pulled me to my feet. "Wish I didn't have to do this," he said. "But I got sloppy leaving that uniform hanging around where you could see it, and well, here we are."

The truth all crashed down then. Jonathan worked for the armored car company that had been robbed. I remembered reading all about it in Miss Smith's newspaper. The uniform I saw in Mr. Butler's apartment was the same one Jonathan wore in the newspaper photo.

I tried to scream but couldn't draw in enough air.

Mr. Butler brought me into the living room and flung me onto the couch. A trail of water puddled behind us. I lay there, too terrified to move, and took in all the things I had always loved: Mom's porcelain angel collection, Mom and Dad's wedding photo, the grandfather clock Gram gave my parents for their tenth wedding anniversary, and the small bust of Abraham Lincoln Dad bought when we visited Washington, DC.

All those things watched silently as I sprawled haphazardly

on Gram's "Home Is Everything" pillow. It had always been one of my favorite things, and I thought about how ironic it was that my home did turn out to be everything to me. It was where I was born and would be the place I died.

When Mr. Butler leaned over me, instinct told me to fight. I scratched his face, digging my short nails into his skin and regretting all the times I bit them down. I punched and kicked like a wild animal, but it didn't make any difference.

That's when I remembered Celia's instruction: ". . . lie still. As still as a dead cat."

A light bulb went on in my head. I forced my arms to go limp. One hung off the couch onto the wooden floor, warm against my knuckles.

After a minute, he exhaled noisily, then walked toward the kitchen. I thought maybe he'd had a change of heart. That maybe a miracle had occurred after all.

"Yeah, there's no use in fighting," he said.

He had no idea fighting for my life had been something I'd become a pro at.

In small movements, I searched beneath the couch, and when something cool and hard brushed against my fingertips, I knew I had found it. I grasped it, and it felt thick and solid in my hand. I had only one chance.

Mr. Butler's cell phone rang again. "Hello?" A few seconds went by before he continued. "Wait, maybe there's another way, we could—" He listened for a bit, then said, "Okay, okay, I'm almost done. No problem, I've got this."

All hope I held on to slipped away.

I watched as he rummaged through the kitchen cabinet for a drinking glass. He snickered when he spotted the three wise monkeys figurine in the sink. "Huh, a monkey statue? Now that's something I've never seen before. It's kind of cool," he said, then stuffed it into his pants pocket. "You won't have any use for it now."

Mr. Butler poured himself some of Mom's iced tea in the mug I'd made her when I made Gram's apron. The mug had my picture on it and the caption read *This Mug's for You*. I watched while he placed his evil mouth on the rim and took a long drink.

He seemed very comfortable, not at all like someone who planned on doing something terrible. He didn't even seem concerned about being caught by my parents. That scared me a lot more than him trying to hurt me, and I hoped with all my might that he'd leave before he got the chance to hurt Mom and Dad too.

Finally, Mr. Butler walked back into the living room. He stopped to look at our family portrait. He stood unmoving for a long time, and I wondered what he thought. Had he changed his mind after all? I fought back the surge of hope that rose in my chest. I needed to be laser focused. My life depended on it.

Somewhere on my block, a car horn blasted, followed by another. It reminded me that life went on as normal, and it always would, with or without me.

Like everything else, this was going to end one way or the other, but I refused to go down easily. I was sick of being scared. Tired of worrying about those I loved. I wanted things to go back to the way they'd always been, and he had no right to keep that from me.

I tightened my grip around what I had found beneath the couch. I only hoped it wouldn't slip from my sweaty palm.

Mr. Butler approached the couch. "I'm sorry," he said as he quickly lifted me to my feet.

"Me too," I said, then slammed the side of his head with the metal bar that had broken loose from the sofa bed. Another thing on Dad's to-do list. If it hadn't been for Julius complaining about how uncomfortable the bed was on the few occasions he slept over, I would've never known about it.

There was a sick metallic thud as the bar made contact.

Mr. Butler stumbled. "Oww!"

It had been a good start, but I still had to get out of there. I dropped the metal bar, then made a dash for the window since it was closer than the front door. Puddles of bathwater made for a slippery sprint.

Just as I pushed out the window screen, Mr. Butler pulled me backward and locked my arms at my sides in a bear hug. I kicked and screamed until my throat was raw and my legs threatened to give out.

The only weapon I had was my hard skull. I jerked my head backward and hoped to connect with his nose.

The blow made a cracking sound. Instantly, Mr. Butler fell to his knees. A gush of bright-red blood exploded from the middle of his shocked face. At last, he crumpled to the floor.

Unfortunately, he blocked the path to the door.

When Mr. Butler bounced back up, I lunged for the metal

bar and clutched it like a baseball bat. The side of his face where I'd first hit him was a swollen wreck. I readied myself for whatever would come next.

I tightened my fingers until they were one with the metal. I wasn't a sports fan, but I aimed to score a home run with the next hit.

I raised my makeshift weapon.

Mr. Butler sprang toward me.

Just as I swung, the front door blasted open behind him.

Julius!

Mr. Butler turned, ducked, and covered his head like he expected the ceiling to collapse. He avoided the hit completely.

Julius grabbed the archangel statue, then hurled it through the air. It hit Mr. Butler squarely in the chest and knocked him to the floor. The hit forced air from his mouth like a popped tire. When he was almost to his feet again, I swung with all my might. I connected with his shoulder and once again sent him to his knees.

Mr. Butler staggered to his feet. He bounced off the doorframe as he went. Defeated and bleeding, he ran out of my house.

Part of me felt like a monster. I'd battered another living thing, but the other part felt like a survivor.

"Tia!" Mrs. Pérez yelled, suddenly standing in the doorway. "Did he hurt you?"

Julius rushed to my side. "Are you okay?"

It took a couple of seconds to take stock of how I felt. I wheezed and my legs shook, but I was okay. "I'm all right," I said, then pumped the extra inhaler I kept on the shelf next to the couch.

"I heard a commotion and got spooked when I came back to check on your eyes. I called 911," Mrs. Pérez said as she quickly checked me over herself. Once satisfied, she hurried to the living room window. "The police should've been here already. He's going to get away!"

"No, he won't," Julius said, halfway out the front door. "I'm going after him."

"But you don't have to, I know where he lives!" I said.

"Exactly, that's why he probably won't go home."

"Well, you're not going without me," I said.

# Chapter Twenty-Seven

Before Mrs. Pérez had the chance to stop us, we hurried out the door and down the block just in time to witness Mr. Butler take a nosedive outside of Tiny's house.

As we got closer, we learned why he had fallen. The sidewalk was wet and soapy. Someone had been cleaning up Tiny's sunflower seed shells.

Mr. Butler lay on his stomach as if he was trying swim away. The monkeys figurine lay on the sidewalk next to him.

We spotted a police car and waved it down. "It was us! We called you!" I said.

The car pulled over, and Detective Erickson, in his own car, was right behind them.

Erickson eyed Mr. Butler. "What's going on?"

That's when the truth flew from my mouth.

"It was him all along!" I said, pointing a finger at Mr. Butler.

Detective Erickson positioned himself in front of Mr. Butler. "What exactly do you mean, Tia?" he said.

I knew I had to confess what I'd witnessed the night of the murder, and now I worried I'd be in trouble for lying about it.

"I saw," I said, after taking a shaky breath, "what happened the night of the murder."

I expected Erickson to scold me, but he just let me talk.

"His name is Mr. Butler, and after he broke into my house, he told me all about the armored car robbery and what happened to Jonathan," I said.

"He tried to . . ." I said. "Hurt me too." I shuddered thinking about what could've happened to me.

Erickson focused completely on me as if no one else was around. His voice was calm and gentle. "Are you okay? Are you injured at all?"

I shook my head, and that's when Erickson pulled Mr. Butler to his feet. Sunflower seed shells stuck to his swollen face. He looked like a giant spotted lizard I once saw at the zoo. His nose was crooked and bloody, and even though he looked pretty pathetic, I had no sympathy for him—none at all. I felt sorry for Potato, though. She'd been the one who lived with a monster.

"But," Julius started, "Detective Erickson, how did you know to come too?"

"I heard the address over the radio."

I don't know what would've happened if Mrs. Pérez hadn't made that call.

I picked up the monkeys figurine, then turned to Mr. Butler. Without a word, I let it drop to the ground, where it shattered.

Just then, Tiny came out of her house. She carried a bucket of water and a scrub brush. She took one look at the chaos and hurried back inside. Maybe her mom didn't let her get away with as much as she had everyone believe.

Erickson removed the metal bar from my clenched fist and that's when I realized not only were my hands shaking, but my whole body was too. Even my kneecaps vibrated. But I was done with being scared, even if my body hadn't caught up yet.

After the EMT gave me a quick checkup, I took a few deep breaths, then filled Erickson in on Mr. Butler's plan to meet someone at Georgie's Diner. I'd learned that it was much more dangerous to stay silent than it was to tell.

"Excellent, excellent," Erickson said, then radioed it all in.

Soon, two more police cars screeched onto our block from opposite directions. Every one of our neighbors rushed out onto the sidewalk to make sure we were okay. Everyone except Miss Smith. She was more interested in Detective Erickson. Whenever he turned his head, she slid out a hair curler and tossed it behind Tiny's metal trash cans. She fluffed and finger combed, and by the time Mr. Butler had been hauled away with his sorry self, Miss Smith looked like she had just gotten out of the hair salon.

Marco skidded to a stop on his bike in front of me. "What happened? Are you all right, Tia?"

"It's a long story, but I'm okay," I said.

He looked down at the porcelain shards of the monkeys figurine. "Oh no, I really wanted you to have that. How did it get broken?"

"What?" I said, confused. "Why?"

"Well," Marco started, "I bought it at a yard sale and thought you'd like it so I–I left it for you."

Julius scowled at him.

I had been so paranoid I never even thought the "warnings" could be innocent. Or more importantly, from a secret admirer. And I was pretty sure that's exactly what Marco was. He had been around more often, and I had seen him watching me, even if I hadn't wanted to acknowledge it.

Still, I had to make absolutely sure. "It was you all along?" I said. "The texts? The chalk?"

When Marco's face reddened, I knew I had my answer.

"Are you serious?" Julius said.

Marco began to pedal away. "I've got to go," he said.

I hadn't meant to embarrass Marco or make him feel bad.

"I'm sorry, T," Julius said. "He must've gotten your number when he borrowed my phone."

Erickson asked where my parents were, and I filled him in on Gram's emergency. Even before I had the chance to ask for a ride to Methodist Hospital, he had already instructed a uniformed police officer to take Julius and me. "First go home and change. You're soaked."

I changed in record time, making it back to the police car in five minutes. Before I climbed into the car I said, "I want to apologize for being such a jerk to you."

Erickson smiled and nodded. "Being under pressure can sometimes make people do things they wouldn't normally do."

That was true in more ways than one, and I wondered if that's what he meant.

Once Julius and I were inside the police car, our hands found each other. It felt good, like we were anchored together in safety. It calmed me in time to face my parents.

Mom had been using the phone at the nurse's station when she spotted us. Her tired eyes mirrored mine. She seemed glad I was there, but when she caught sight of the police officer behind Julius, her smile evaporated. She dropped the phone onto the desk and knocked a stack of papers to the floor.

I let her hug me, then Julius. "We're okay, Mom," I said.

Mom pulled away and inspected us. "What in the world is going on? Why is there a policeman with you?"

The policeman stepped in and told Mom not to worry, that he'd explain everything to her.

"Mom, what happened to Gram?" I said.

"The doctors think she may have had a stroke."

My heart sank until I was sure it had hit the bottom of my stomach. "Could she die?"

"There's a good chance she was brought in before anything . . ."

Mom didn't finish her thought, and I didn't push. I couldn't, not with Mom crying the way she was. Not with the way I cried too.

Mom turned her attention to the police officer, who began to explain everything that had happened, which almost pushed her over the edge. It was only after I assured her that I wasn't hurt that she allowed me to peek in on Gram.

While Mom continued to speak to the officer, I folded my hand around Julius's and together we walked to the double doors of the ER, where we peered in through the small window that led inside.

There was nothing to see but blue curtains closed around small cubicles. Doctors and nurses rushed from one to the other.

"Look," Julius said. "I can see Gram right there on that bed."

I stretched up on my toes to get a better look, but still didn't see her. "Where?"

Julius tapped his long, skinny finger against the glass. "There," he said. "Right next to the nurse with the blond hair."

Finally, I got a glimpse of Gram, but I wished I hadn't. She looked too small to be my gram. At her side, Dad held her hand.

Dad joined us after a few minutes. He wasn't the Dad I knew. His face was tense, and his shoulders slumped.

He squeezed me tightly. "Hi, baby," he said.

I held on to him. "How's Gram?" I said. "Is she going to be okay?"

He placed his hand on Julius's shoulder. "We just don't know yet," he said.

Just then someone called out.

When the man reached us, Dad said, "Hey, Sal, what're you doing here?"

"I was going to ask you the same question."

Dad motioned toward the double doors and sighed. "It's my mother. She's had a stroke. They brought her in a little while ago."

"Oh no! I'm so sorry to hear that," Sal said.

Dad introduced me to Sal. He shook my hand, then Julius's.

"What's with the security guard uniform?" Dad asked.

"I needed a second job. I applied a few months ago, and when they called me in last minute, I jumped on it. Just in time, too. I really have to get my own apartment. One with no roommate and quieter neighbors. The extra money can help with that."

"That's great. I'm happy for you," Dad said.

"Listen, I'm not supposed to do this," Sal said. "Rule says only one visitor at a time, but since it's you, you can bring your daughter and her friend in to see her." He held out two visitor passes.

"Are you sure?" Dad said. "I don't want you to get into trouble."

"You're like family to me. It'll be okay."

Dad hugged Sal. "Thank you so much."

I was glad to see that Dad had a true friend in Sal and felt silly when I thought about how I suspected him to be the killer.

"Nice to meet you," I said.

Sal smiled. "Same here."

Dad handed us the passes. "You two go ahead. I'm going to find Mom," he said.

I was relieved to know I didn't have to fill Dad in on Mr. Butler. Mom would take care of that. All I wanted to do at that moment was see Gram.

Once we were through the doors of the ER, Julius led me straight to Gram's bedside. We weren't sure if she was asleep or not, so just in case, we kept quiet.

The blue hospital gown Gram wore hung loose from her shoulders. Small, round electrodes were stuck to her rising and falling chest in various places. The wires attached to them snaked back to a monitor, which beeped every couple of seconds. A clear plastic mask wet with condensation fit snugly over her delicate nose and lips.

Gram's sunken mouth made her appear much older than she was. I knew it was because they'd removed her dentures. I half smiled and thought about how mad she'd be if she knew what they'd done. Gram never let anyone see her without her teeth in.

I lightly kissed Gram's cool, clammy forehead and hoped she'd open her eyes and tell me she was fine, but she didn't. Not even an eyelid fluttered in recognition.

Julius wiped his eyes with the back of his hand. "I'd better call my parents to let them know where I am. I'll be right back."

I gently touched Gram's arm where clear tape held an IV needle in place. Her soft skin folded and wrinkled beneath it.

I sat on the cold fake-leather chair beside Gram's bed and cried quietly. Seeing Gram like that, along with what I had just gone through, was too much.

Outside of Gram's curtained cubicle, life moved along as usual. Nurses made dinner plans, people smiled and discussed vacation plans. But I wanted them to be sad and silent. Like I was.

A few minutes later Julius came back with my parents. We all squeezed into the small space around Gram's bed. By the look on Dad's face, I knew Mom had told him all about what happened with Mr. Butler. He lifted me from the chair and gently held me. My cheek grew wet with his tears.

"I'm so, so sorry, baby," Dad said. "Are you sure you're all right?"

"Yeah, but Mr. Butler isn't. I bet he's sorry he ever messed with me. Plus, as a going-away present, Julius lobbed the statue Gram bought from the botanica at him. It knocked the air right out of him."

Dad looked over at Gram. "I guess you were right, Mami. The statue was for protection after all."

Through our tears, we laughed.

# Chapter Twenty-Eight

Gram was finally moved from the ER into a room in the intensive care unit. Mom, Julius, and I stayed at the hospital until almost midnight, when we got kicked out. Dad was allowed to stay, and Mom promised to relieve him first thing the next morning.

Detective Erickson and two other policemen waited for us when we got home. They had picked up Mr. Butler's partner, Mack, who was a waiter at Georgie's Diner, and both he and Mr. Butler had been taken into custody.

I remembered seeing Mack at the memorial when I first met Mr. Butler. They were both bold enough to return to the scene.

"This is what we know as of right now," Erickson said. "Since Jonathan worked for the armored car company, he knew the routes and routines and could set up the robbery with little trouble, even steal extra uniforms for his partners, which made it easier to move undetected."

"When it was done," Erickson continued, "Jonathan announced his plan to give his share of the money to charity."

That didn't surprise me at all. It was too bad he didn't stick to helping others in the right way—legally.

"But Jonathan's partners worried giving away such a hefty

sum would bring too much attention and they'd all get caught. The night of the murder, Butler met Jonathan at the House of Pizza, where Butler tried talking him out of it, but he wouldn't budge."

I remembered Mr. Butler saying Jonathan never showed up that night. How I wished it had been true. If Jonathan hadn't gone, maybe he'd be alive.

"Mack had spent time in jail a couple of years ago," Erickson continued, "and had no intention to go back on a murder rap. As you can imagine, it didn't take long for him to roll over on Butler, who had planned the whole thing."

"Man," Julius said, "sounds like stuff that happens in the movies."

Detective Erickson looked first at me, then Mom. "Tia, will you be willing to testify against Mr. Butler?"

That was something I hadn't thought about, and I wasn't sure I could do it.

But Mr. Butler had taken Jonathan's life and tried to take mine too. He had controlled me and made me afraid. I decided not to give him the chance to control me any longer.

Mom began to say something, but I didn't give her a chance to finish.

I took Mom's hand. "Yes," I said. "You can count on me."

On his way out, Erickson stopped and said, "It was odd— when we searched Butler's place, it was filled with dog toys and other pet paraphernalia, but no dog."

"What?" I said. "I know for a fact he had a dog. I've even walked her."

"We searched everywhere," Erickson said. "No pup."

"She must've gotten out somehow," Julius offered.

My stomach ached at the thought of Potato as she wandered the streets alone and frightened. I hoped that she'd be protected somehow, some way.

After everyone left, Mom checked the messages on the answering machine. Three were from Erickson, one had been from my dad's boss telling him they'd caught the thief at the factory on camera and it had been Mr. Hernandez after all. He'd led the police to where he had hidden the money. It was at the abandoned car dealership where we'd run into him. The last message was about me.

"Hello, this is Mia calling on behalf of Camp Troy. I noticed there was a last-minute cancellation and wanted to reach out to let you know that due to the high rate of interest in this program, we've added a second week to accommodate more campers. If the added week works better for your schedule, I encourage you to sign up. Since you're already in our system, you'll receive priority admittance. I hope you decide to join us at Camp Troy for a truly unforgettable summer."

Calling this an unforgettable summer was the understatement of the year.

"Do you still want to go?" Mom said.

"How could I with Gram . . . ?"

Mom put her warm hand to my cheek. "Gram would want you to, but you don't have to make a decision tonight. Let's give it until tomorrow, okay?"

I nodded.

Mom hugged me like I'd just received an award and, in a way, maybe I had. I had learned how to survive amid brick buildings and concrete; next, maybe I'd conquer the outdoors at camp.

Mrs. Pérez must've been watching for us to return, because after Erickson left, it was only a couple of minutes before she came over. She wore her pajamas and a monogrammed lavender robe. We all sat at the kitchen table, exhausted.

Mrs. Pérez took my face in her hands. "I'm so glad you're safe. That man is going to rot in prison for the terrible things he's done."

Mom held on to my hand across the table. No words were needed; her face said it all.

"I hope you don't mind," Mrs. Pérez continued, "but I cleaned up a little. I didn't think it was right for you to have to come home to such craziness."

I'd been so thankful to Mrs. Pérez that I hugged her a good long while. She'd saved my parents from the grief of having to see evidence of my near-death experience.

Mom thanked her about a hundred times.

After Mrs. Pérez left, Mom called an emergency locksmith to replace our broken back-door lock right away. When that was done, I collapsed into bed with Mom, but couldn't sleep. I wasn't surprised, especially with poor Potato on my mind. But still, I longed for the days when my parents' bed seemed magical. Always able to shoo away bad dreams, its power hadn't been strong enough to chase away reality. I had lived a bad dream, and that wasn't the same as simply having one made from random pieces of your imagination.

---

The next morning, Mom and Dad traded places at the hospital.

When Dad got home, his face was scruffy. Puffy bags sat beneath his tired eyes.

I made scrambled eggs and toast for breakfast. Scrambled is the only way I was able to make eggs without burning them. But even if I had burned them, Dad was so hungry he probably would've eaten them anyway.

"Mom told me about camp. Gram's a fighter, you know," Dad said between mouthfuls. "Even the doctors were surprised by the progress she'd made during the night. I'm pretty sure it'll be okay if you go. And besides . . ."

"Gram would want me to go," I finished.

Dad took my hand and gave it a squeeze. I squeezed back.

When I had cleaned up breakfast, I joined Dad on the couch.

"Tia," Dad started. "I need you to know that you can come to us with anything. You never have to do hard things alone. Ever."

My throat grew tight and made it hard to speak. I nodded and we hugged.

After a little while Dad fell fast asleep. I cuddled up next to him and closed my eyes. For just a little while, I forgot all about Mr. Butler. I was with Dad, and I was safe.

Except for the ticking of the clock, the house was quiet as Dad slept.

I covered Dad, then as quietly as I could, I hauled my suitcase into the middle of my bedroom floor. It was still packed but I wanted to double-check that I had everything I'd need for camp. A folded piece of paper peeked out from between the clothes.

Dear T,

I can't wait for you to come back and you haven't even left yet! You know I'm happy for you though. You're getting to do something you've been wanting to do since forever. I have no idea what I'm going to do without you for a whole week. Well, maybe I do. I'll be missing you, that's what.

Anyway, remember everything you learn at camp so you can teach it to me. There's nobody I'd rather survive a zombie apocalypse with than you.

From,

Jul

So that had been why Julius offered to bring my suitcase downstairs. I sat with the letter on my lap for a long time, then kissed it and put it into an empty shoebox. It was the very first item added to my newly declared memento box.

Later that day, Mom and Dad went with me to the police station, where I gave an official statement of what happened. Each held on to me in one way or another as I went over the scariest day of my life. It was their way of letting me know they'd never let me go, and I was so glad for that.

When we got back, Dad lit the candle on the front table, then closed his eyes. I knew he was praying for Gram, and maybe even for me. When he was done, I joined him and together we watched as the flame grew tall and strong. Like my family. Like me.

# Epilogue

Smoke from Mrs. Pérez's wood-burning fireplace permeated the crisp air. The hem of my black-and-red robe rustled the fallen leaves as I walked.

Our neighborhood was bursting with excited activity. Everywhere I looked, candy wrappers littered the sidewalks. It was my job to sweep up any that found their way to the front of our house.

I'd wanted to skip Halloween, but Julius talked me into dressing up, and since it had been too late to buy something new, we both dug out our old zombie wizard costumes. We did away with the zombie part, though. After what I'd been through just a few months earlier, gruesome was not on our list, and probably would never be again, at least not for me.

"But you love Halloween," Julius said in his argument to get me to dress up.

He was right. Halloween had always been my favorite time of the year. I couldn't let Mr. Butler take that—or anything else—away from me. If I had, it would've been like giving him permission to rule over my life like some evil lord. So, I joined Julius in search of free candy, the same as I always had.

Potato stood on her hind legs and begged to be picked

up, as usual. We'd become inseparable ever since I'd found her wandering the neighborhood, wet and dirty. As soon as I spotted her, I knew we were meant to be. I pleaded with my parents to give her a chance, and once they saw her, it was a done deal. I never found out how she escaped from Mr. Butler's apartment, but it didn't matter. She was mine, and I'd never let her out of my sight.

After Gram had her stroke, the right side of her body was very weak, and she had trouble walking. But with physical therapy five days a week, the doctors were optimistic that she'd walk again one day. Dad and Sal built a ramp so Gram's wheelchair could easily navigate the front steps into the house. Then, they moved Gram in with us so she'd never be alone. We carved out a space for her in our living room, and almost every night Gram and I ate popcorn and watched a romantic movie. Even Mom and Dad usually joined us.

I took up brushing Gram's hair just before she got into bed each night. Gram insisted the living arrangement was only temporary, but I hoped she'd never leave us.

Now Gram sat on our stoop in her chair, watching the little ghosts, goblins, and superheroes run wild. A warm fleece blanket draped across her lap protected her from the cool October breeze. She wore a witch's hat and directed the trick-or-treaters to take two pieces of candy each. Once they made their choices, Gram handed every child a new book from the stack by her side. Just a week before, she sent me and Julius to the dollar store to buy the books. The kids loved them as much as we loved picking them out. When Dad saw how much joy the books brought to everyone, he announced that come spring, he'd install a Little Free Library outside of our house. Julius and I would be in charge of designing it, and we couldn't wait to get started.

Marco, who had not bothered to wear a costume, rounded the corner with a bulging pillowcase and headed straight for us. He must've hit every house in our neighborhood. Danielle walked beside him. She wore a sparkly pink top and shiny gold pants. Attached to her shoulders was a pair of purple wings. Her makeup was awesome. Pink and green shimmered across her eyelids and extended toward her temples. Lips the same shade of gold as her pants glittered in a wide smile. A rainbow crown sat high on top of her teased hair.

Julius pointed to Danielle. "What're you supposed to be?" he said.

"A fairy princess," Danielle and I said together, then laughed.

Marco shifted the pillowcase from one hand to the other without so much as a glance toward me, and I was grateful for that. After the "gift" and messages he'd left for me, things had been awkward, but I knew it would fade away and become just another stitch in the fabric of our neighborhood.

Julius pointed to the pillowcase. "You have enough candy?" he said

"It's not all mine." Marco looked to Danielle. "It's ours."

Julius pointed from Danielle to Marco and grinned. "Ohhh," he said.

Danielle took Marco's free hand.

"Hey where's your little shadow, Tiny?" Julius said.

"No clue," Danielle said as they began to walk away. "See you later, Tia."

It felt good to be called by my name and not Priestess Junior. "Bye, Danielle," I said.

I scooped up Potato and adjusted the miniature pink tutu Mom put together for her. Every little kid—and almost every adult—we encountered wanted to pet her, and she loved the attention.

Julius consulted the compass I'd given him. I knew he'd like using one as much as I had at survival camp, so I bought him one. "Due east," he said, pointing to the next house on our route.

That made me giggle. Julius was never without his compass and that made me feel good.

"So," Julius said when he walked me home, "the Autumn Dance is next week. Want to go with me?"

I felt that familiar slight flutter in my stomach. Even though we'd been "official" for a month, it still felt brand-new to me.

I stood on my tiptoes and kissed his warm, soft cheek. "Absolutely."

Julius grinned. "See," he said. "No love potion needed."

That made me think of the botanica and all it had to offer. Maybe sometimes people need to feel connected to something bigger and stronger than themselves. Even something magical. I know that's how I felt after the murder. Maybe people visit the botanica hoping to find just the thing they need to find peace. But the truth is, you can't buy magic or strength. Those things are inside all of us, and I won't ever forget that.

# Acknowledgments

A huge thank-you to Jolly Fish Press for giving me the incredible opportunity to introduce the world to Tia and her family. Much love especially to Mari Kesselring for giggling in all the right spots and for being one of the nicest people I've ever had the pleasure of working with. A true partner.

# About the Author

Danette Vigilante grew up in the Red Hook Houses in Brooklyn, New York. She now resides in Staten Island with her family, sweet pup, and an elderly cat who has just learned to meow. Danette is the author of *The Trouble with a Half Moon*, a 2012–2013 Sunshine State Young Readers Award nominee, and *Saving Baby Doe*, a 2014 pick for the New York Public Library's 100 Titles for Reading and Sharing list. Danette encourages literacy in her community via a Little Free Library installed on her front lawn.